"What's wrong?" Neil asked. When Andy didn't say anything, Neil looked into his friend's locker to see what the problem was. He felt his stomach drop.

Andy's locker was full of cafeteria garbage. It was a complete mess.

"What the—!" Neil exclaimed. Then he noticed something was written on the inside of the locker door: "Go back to Africa where you belong."

"Andy—I can't believe this," Neil whispered, horrified.

Andy drew a deep breath, then let out a hollow laugh. "It's no big deal," he said, obviously trying to sound nonchalant.

"But, you mean, you're just going to ignore it?" Neil asked.

"What do you want me to do?" Andy asked. "Yell racism and go running to the principal? That's just what they want, whoever did this."

"Look," Neil said. "I really think you should tell Mr. Cooper about this."

Andy shook his head decisively. "Let me handle it my own way, Neil. I just think it's better not to get all confrontational about it."

Reluctantly, Neil nodded. Maybe his friend was right. Maybe it was better to let it pass. But deep down, he knew that ignoring the problem wouldn't make it go away.

Bantam Books in the Sweet Valley High Series
Ask your bookseller for the books you have missed

SWEET VALLEY HIGH

FRIEND AGAINST FRIEND

Written by
Kate William

Created by
FRANCINE PASCAL

BANTAM BOOKS
NEW YORK · TORONTO · LONDON · SYDNEY · AUCKLAND

RL6, IL age 12 and up

FRIEND AGAINST FRIEND
A Bantam Book / October 1990

Sweet Valley High is a registered trademark of Francine Pascal

Conceived by Francine Pascal

Produced by Daniel Weiss Associates, Inc.
33 West 17th Street
New York, NY 10011

Cover art by James Mathewuse

ISBN 0-553-28636-6

Published simultaneously in the United States and Canada

Bantam Books are published by Bantam Books, a division of Bantam Doubleday
Dell Publishing Group, Inc. Its trademark, consisting of the words "Bantam
Books" and the portrayal of a rooster, is Registered in U.S. Patent and Trademark
Office and in other countries. Marca Registrada. Bantam Books, 666 Fifth Avenue,
New York, New York 10103

PRINTED IN THE UNITED STATES OF AMERICA

OPM   0 9 8 7 6 5 4 3 2 1

One

"I'm so hungry I think I might pass out," Jessica Wakefield said in a dismal voice. It was Friday afternoon, and she had just gotten out of her last class. She leaned against a locker and closed her eyes.

Elizabeth, her identical twin sister, was not overly concerned. Jessica made an average of six melodramatic statements every day.

"Didn't you eat lunch?" Elizabeth asked as she took the books she needed for the weekend out of her locker.

Jessica opened one eye. "You know perfectly well I'm on a diet, Liz. I can hardly get into my cheerleading uniform."

Nothing could be further from the truth, Elizabeth reflected. Like Elizabeth, Jessica had a perfect size-six figure. Add to that sun-streaked blond hair, eyes the blue-green of the Pacific Ocean, and a lovely heart-shaped face, and the Wakefield twins ended up as two of the prettiest girls at Sweet Valley High. In every way they looked absolutely identical, right down to the dimples in their left cheeks.

But the similarity ended there. Elizabeth was more responsible, thoughtful, and dependable than her whirlwind twin. Elizabeth wanted to be a writer some day, so she spent much of her free time reading, writing in her journal, or working on the school newspaper, *The Oracle*. Jessica was just the opposite: She craved excitement, and didn't mind stirring things up just to see the sparks fly. She went from hobby to hobby, from boyfriend to boyfriend, with lightning speed. But no matter what kind of trouble she got herself into, she always knew she could turn to Elizabeth for help.

"Are you staying after school to work on the paper?" Jessica asked.

"Yes," Elizabeth said, snapping her locker door shut and turning the combination lock. She gave her twin a smile. "Pick me up after cheerleading, OK? I'll wait on the front steps."

Jessica slung her pink gym bag over her shoulder. "OK. Hey, Liz, can you lend me some change? I need a candy bar or something."

Some diet, Elizabeth thought. She handed Jessica two quarters, then watched her walk down the hall. As Jessica disappeared around a corner, Elizabeth noticed the *Oracle*'s editor-in-chief, Penny Ayala, coming toward her.

"Hi, Pen!" Elizabeth called.

Penny waved, and the two girls fell into step together.

"I had an idea for the paper," Elizabeth said as they headed for the *Oracle* office. "It's a survey. We ask the question, 'If you could change anything at Sweet Valley High, what would it be?' Then we tell people to write in their responses, and we can publish the most interesting suggestions. Who knows? Maybe some of the changes can actually be made. What do you think?"

Penny cocked her head to one side. "I think it's a good idea. That could be really fun, especially if we get a lot of people involved. Let's try it out on Mr. Collins and see what he thinks. If we catch him today, there'll be just enough time to make sure it goes in Monday's paper."

As the two girls walked down the hallway,

Penny's expression changed from thoughtful to happy, and her hazel eyes brightened.

Elizabeth followed Penny's gaze and saw that Neil Freemount, a tall, blond, good-looking boy, was coming toward them.

Penny and Neil had started dating when Neil answered a personal ad that Penny had placed in *The Oracle*. Although their relationship had gotten off to a rocky start, they were now very much in love. They were one of Elizabeth's favorite Sweet Valley High couples.

"Hi," Neil said, walking up and slipping his arm around Penny's shoulders. "I'm staying late to work on this lab for marine biology," he told them. "Andy and I are going for extra credit."

"Great. Say hi to Andy," Penny said as Neil continued on down the hall.

"Neil is Andy Jenkins's lab partner?" Elizabeth asked, raising her eyebrows. "Lucky Neil."

Andy Jenkins was one of the best science students at Sweet Valley High. He had won certificates of merit in biology and chemistry, and he had won the all-county science fair twice.

"They've gotten to be good friends," Penny answered.

Elizabeth nodded. Andy was one of a few black students in the school. She didn't know him very well, but she liked what she knew about him. He seemed to be easy-going and friendly, and he got along with everyone. Besides being a science whiz, Andy played the French horn in the school orchestra, and he was a guitarist in a band called Baja Beat. Baja Beat wasn't as popular or well-known at Sweet Valley High as the rock group The Droids, but Elizabeth really liked their music. The school had recently sponsored a "Battle of the Bands," and Baja Beat had been stiff competition for The Droids, even though The Droids had won.

"Well, I'm not surprised they're friends," Elizabeth said with a teasing grin. "Neil obviously has very good taste and judgment. After all, he's going out with you, right?"

"Right." Penny laughed. "Come on. If we're going to find out what needs to be changed at school, we have to get started."

Elizabeth followed Penny into the *Oracle* office.

"Penny! Liz!" called out Olivia Davidson, the arts editor. "You didn't bring any food, did you?"

Elizabeth laughed. "Everyone's hungry today," she joked, putting her books down. She sat down across from Olivia and put her elbows on the table. "Listen, if you could change any-

5

thing at all at school—*anything*—what would it be?"

"That's easy," Olivia began. "I'd cut the school week to three days and have homework outlawed!"

Elizabeth and Penny laughed.

"Seriously, though," Penny said, "there *is* something I would change."

Elizabeth looked at her. "What's that?" she asked.

"I'd get rid of the sorority, Pi Beta Alpha," Penny said. "I know you're in it, Liz. . . ."

Elizabeth was somewhat surprised. She had no idea that Penny felt that way. "Just out of habit," she hastened to say. She had joined because Jessica had begged her to.

"It sets up this exclusivity thing," Penny continued. "I don't think that's the kind of attitude we really want in our school. You're in or you're out. That's just not right."

Olivia nodded. "I agree." Turning to Elizabeth, she said, "Why did you want to know, anyway?"

"Well, I had this idea to do a survey in the paper," she explained to Olivia. "I thought we could ask kids what they'd like to see changed at school. Then we can run some of the answers."

Privately, Elizabeth had thought of it as just a fun thing to do. More soft drink machines, shorter classes, better food in the cafeteria: those were the responses she had expected. But maybe there was more dissatisfaction at Sweet Valley High than she thought.

"What is this stuff, anyway?" Neil joked. He held up a bottle of slimy-looking liquid. "I don't even want to say what this looks like."

Andy's muscular frame was hunched over his lab notebook, his handsome face knit in concentration as he wrote up some observations. "It looks like the stuff inside your head," he said after a moment. When he looked up, his brown eyes had a devilish twinkle in them.

"Oh, yeah, Jenkins?" Neil held the bottle over Andy's head. "Are you sure you don't want to change your mind?"

"Oh, what I meant was, it's the control bottle of brine water from the marina," Andy explained in a mock-terrified voice.

Neil nodded sagely. "That's what I thought you meant."

"Come on," said Andy, laughing. "Let's get through this experiment."

They worked steadily for half an hour. Even

though they still joked around, they were both serious about the lab work. Together, they tested bottles of water from different locations along the coast for salt content, pollution, and microorganisms. Neil was grateful to have such a good partner.

And as he watched Andy carefully measure water into a beaker, he thought about how glad he was that they had become friends. When they were assigned as partners, he didn't know Andy very well. But now they spent a lot of time together, and he and Penny often double-dated with Andy and his girlfriend, Tracy Gilbert. Tracy was also a junior at Sweet Valley High.

"This water from the marina is really bad," Andy said in a disappointed tone. He shook his head. "There has to be some way to have a marina without destroying the environment around it."

"Yeah," Neil agreed. "If only we could figure out how. I don't even like swimming in the ocean anymore. You never really know what's in it."

"Hey, speaking of swimming," Andy said, "Tracy and I are going to the beach on Saturday. Why don't you and Penny come? We can

8

take a picnic, play Frisbee. You don't have to swim if you don't want."

Neil made a face. "Sorry, I can't. My folks are having this family picnic thing with some friends, and I have to be there."

"Hey, no problem," Andy told him. "Maybe some other time."

In another fifteen minutes they were finished with the experiment. While they cleaned up, they talked about a suspense movie that had just come out that they both wanted to see.

As they headed for their lockers, Neil asked, "Need a ride home?"

"Sure. Mind if we stop by the music room for a minute?" Andy said, stopping at his locker and working his combination. "I have to pick up my horn. There's this—"

He broke off suddenly as he opened the door. He looked stunned.

"What's wrong?" Neil asked. When Andy didn't say anything, Neil looked into his friend's locker to see what the problem was. Then Neil felt his stomach drop.

Andy's locker was full of cafeteria garbage: soda cans; apple cores; crumpled, dirty paper; pizza crusts. It was a complete mess.

"What the—!" Neil exclaimed. Then he noticed something was written on the inside of the locker door: "Go back to Africa where you belong."

"Andy—I can't believe this," Neil whispered, horrified.

Andy drew a deep breath, then let out a hollow laugh. "It's no big deal," he said, obviously trying to sound nonchalant. "This kind of stuff—it's so stupid, how can you even pay attention to it?" He started pulling the garbage out and throwing it into a nearby wastebasket.

"But—you mean, you're just going to ignore it?" Neil asked. He couldn't believe this had happened. Somebody had gone to a lot of trouble to do this to Andy. He didn't want to believe it was just because Andy was black. But obviously it was. The message made that perfectly clear. He felt embarrassed, ashamed, and angry that it had happened in his school, to his friend.

"Andy, you have to—" Neil began.

"What do you want me to do?" Andy cut in. "Yell racism and go running to the principal? That's just what they want, whoever did this. Besides, maybe it's just someone who doesn't like my horn playing."

Neil shook his head. He could tell that underneath his casual attitude, his friend was shaken up. "How can you joke about it?"

10

"It's better than banging my head against a wall," Andy said dryly.

"Look," Neil said. "I really think you should tell Mr. Cooper about this. You can't let whoever did this get away with it."

Andy curled his lip in disgust as he wiped his hands off on a dirty napkin. He shook his head decisively. "Let me handle it my own way, Neil. I just think it's better not to get all confrontational about it."

"But—"

"Just drop it, OK?" Andy broke in. "If I make a big deal out of it, things will just get worse. Maybe if I let it go, these jokers won't bother me again."

Reluctantly, Neil nodded. Maybe his friend was right. Maybe it was better to let it pass.

But deep down, he knew that ignoring the problem wouldn't make it go away.

Two

Neil drove to Penny's house on Saturday morning. She had been out with some girlfriends the night before, so he hadn't been able to tell her about the incident at Andy's locker, and he needed to talk it over with her. Penny met him at the door with a big smile, but when she saw his expression, she frowned.

"What's up?" she asked, leading the way into the living room.

Neil perched on the arm of the sofa. "Don't tell Andy I told you this," he began. "Yesterday, after we finished our lab work, we stopped at his locker, right?"

"Go on." Penny was watching him intently.

"So when he opened it, it was full of garbage," Neil continued. "And there was this note that said 'Go back to Africa.' "

"What?" she gasped. "How did it happen? Who could have done that?"

"I don't know," Neil said. "But Andy just wants to drop the whole thing, and that doesn't seem right."

"Of course he can't," Penny went on in an outraged voice. Her hazel eyes flashed with indignation. "You can't just ignore something like that. It's racism, pure and simple, and it won't just go away. We have to tell Mr. Cooper, tell as many people as we can. Maybe if everyone stands up for Andy, whoever did it will back off. The whole thing is outrageous."

"That what I said. But Andy doesn't want to make a big thing of it," Neil said. "He says that will only make the creep who did it want to do more."

"Well, that's probably true," Penny admitted grudgingly. She ran her fingers through her short dark blond hair and frowned. "But it still seems wrong to let the jerk get away with it. Shouldn't we—"

"I think it's his decision," Neil cut in. "I felt the same way as you. But after thinking about it I decided that I don't have the right to complain

13

about it if Andy doesn't want me to. It happened to him, not to us. But it makes me feel pretty helpless, you know?"

Penny moved closer to him and took his hand. "You're right. It's Andy's decision."

"I just wish I knew who did it," Neil grumbled, making a fist. "I would definitely have something to say to that jerk."

"Andy's right, Neil," Penny cut in. "You can't talk to people like that. They don't listen to reason."

Neil sank back against the couch and looked up at the ceiling. "I know. Anyway, I can't stay very long because of that family picnic with the Cashmans."

"Poor you," Penny said sympathetically. "Charlie is a total Neanderthal."

Charlie Cashman was known for being a bully. He always chose the weakest member of a group to tease and taunt and play dirty tricks on. His father and Mr. Freemount were good friends, and they worked together at Patman Canning on the outskirts of Sweet Valley. So Neil and Charlie were thrown together at family gatherings. Nothing could force Neil to like Charlie, however. They said hello in the halls at school, but except for the family get-togethers, they didn't hang around with each other. They didn't have any friends in common, either.

"Yeah, well, I'm only staying as long as I have to," Neil said in a tired voice. "I can't stand Charlie or his father. Mom says I have to be there, though. Ever since Gary left for college, I'm always getting stuck at these family events." Neil's older brother was a freshman at UCLA.

Penny gave him a tender smile. "Will you call me later?"

"Sure." Neil stood up and gave her a hug. "When I escape."

"I can make an emergency call," Penny suggested, smiling up at him. "Say I need urgent help opening a can of soda."

"Great idea," Neil said and gave Penny a long kiss before heading for the door.

When Neil arrived back at his house, his mother asked him to mow the lawn and clean the picnic table, while Mr. Freemount tinkered with the charcoal grill. Shortly before lunchtime, Mr. and Mrs. Cashman arrived with a bowl of potato salad and a cake.

"Charlie couldn't make it," Marge Cashman explained with an apologetic smile as they all went to the backyard. "He said to say hi, Neil."

Neil smiled politely.

15

"So, you didn't go out for football this year, did you Neil?" Frank Cashman said in a big, hearty voice. "It's a great character builder."

"Neil plays tennis," Mrs. Freemount reminded him. "And soccer."

"Soccer? Oh, right—never cared for it, myself. That's what those South Americans play. I don't trust those guys."

Mr. Cashman walked away and sat down at the picnic table with Neil's father, while Neil stared at him in disbelief.

"Why don't you get Mr. and Mrs. Cashman some iced tea," Mrs. Freemount whispered to Neil.

Nodding, Neil hurried into the house. He was more than happy to get away from Frank Cashman. He already felt impatient and frustrated. Mr. Cashman was a perfect example of what Charlie would be like in twenty-five years: overbearing, loud-mouthed, and insensitive. And Mrs. Cashman was always so timid that Neil couldn't say anything without flustering her. But he only had to stay a little while, he reminded himself. It wouldn't kill him. He poured two tall glasses of iced tea and carried them out to the backyard.

"That's right, I knew just what the problem was," Mr. Cashman was saying. He took his

16

iced tea without a word to Neil and took a big swallow. "I told him, your distributor cap is loose, and of course, that's what it was."

"You should have been an auto mechanic," Carol Freemount said as she handed him the potato chips.

"Could have been," Mr. Cashman said confidently. "The jokers these days that pass for mechanics—they don't know a thing. It's pathetic. Any time I have to take my car somewhere, I have to spell it out for them what's wrong and what to do. And they still screw around checking for things that aren't even there. Just to stick me with a huge bill."

Neil fiddled with the plastic knives and forks. "I'll check the burgers," he offered, standing up abruptly.

Going over to the grill, he stared moodily at the smoldering embers. When he compared five minutes in Penny's company to five minutes in Mr. Cashman's, he felt even worse about having to stay for the picnic.

Snatches of the adults' conversation drifted over to him as he flipped the hamburgers. His father and Mr. Cashman seemed to be complaining about someone at work.

"I had a feeling this would happen," Neil's

father said. "As soon as he got that promotion, he started holding it over us."

"No kidding," Mr. Cashman agreed. "Willis is too big for his britches. Of course, people like that always let power go to their heads. Can't handle it."

"Why? What does he do?" Neil's mother asked.

Frank Cashman snorted. "Mainly he's got this thing about punctuality. To the minute. You can be a lousy fifteen minutes late, and he acts like you're committing a crime. I mean, I always figure, you do your work, what difference does it make if you're a little late sometimes? Big deal."

"Isn't punctuality important?" Mrs. Cashman put in nervously.

"Don't be a fool, Marge," Mr. Cashman told her. "The thing is, he's getting totally carried away. He never would have gotten the job if it weren't for this stupid affirmative-action thing, anyway. There were plenty of regular guys who were in line for that promotion. Talk about discrimination!"

Neil stopped poking at the hamburgers and was very still. He listened more intently.

"I think you have a point there," Paul Freemount said. "I'm not a hundred percent sure Willis deserved that job."

"Why not?" his wife put in sharply. "Isn't he qualified?"

"Oh, sure," Neil's father said. "I mean, as much as you can expect from someone like that."

Neil swallowed hard. "Like what, Dad?" he asked in a loud voice.

Neil's parents and the Cashmans turned in surprise to look at him. Neil's father looked uncomfortable. "Oh—well, what I meant was—"

Mrs. Freemount frowned. "I'm not sure I follow you, Frank," she said in a warning tone. "What exactly do you mean by 'someone like that'?"

"Oh, come on now," Mr. Cashman said. "They're just different, that's all. We all know it's true."

Neil's face was burning. "There's nothing different about—"

Mr. Freemount spoke up. "All we're really saying is, it's not his fault if he was disadvantaged as a kid, but this affirmative-action thing isn't fair. I don't have anything against black people. Lots of them are really nice. Like your friend, Andy. He's a smart guy, and he works hard."

"Yeah, he does," Neil said. He couldn't meet his father's eyes.

Was his father saying Andy was an exception to the rule? If so, then what was the rule—that black people were mostly lazy and stupid?

I thought that went out in the sixties, Neil thought in astonishment. *That's not what Dad meant. It couldn't be.*

Obviously, Mr. Cashman felt that Willis was difficult to work for because of his race. Neil couldn't believe his father felt the same way, but then again, he wasn't sure.

Marge Cashman cleared her throat. "Did you know we were thinking of getting a motor boat. Frank and Charlie are very excited about it. It has—"

"Let me tell it," her husband interrupted her. "You should see this baby. Fifteen feet long, fiberglass, built for speed. She's a beauty."

Deeply troubled, Neil turned back to the hamburgers. He liked to think that his father was fair. But if he spent so much time with Mr. Cashman, some of those bigoted attitudes might rub off on him. Attitudes like Mr. Cashman's were the reason people like Andy got their lockers trashed.

He stole a quick glance at his mother to see how she was reacting to the conversation. The look she was giving Mr. Cashman was not exactly friendly.

"How are those burgers coming along, Neil?" Mr. Cashman called out.

"They're ready," Neil muttered, lifting the burgers off the grill and putting them on a platter.

For the rest of the meal, the conversation was basically neutral. But Neil couldn't help reading racist overtones into almost everything Mr. Cashman said. He kept seeing Andy's face and thinking how his friend would react if he could hear some of the stuff that was being said. By the time lunch was over, Neil felt as if he couldn't stand another minute of it.

As soon as the Cashmans left, Neil went upstairs to his room and slammed the door. Lying on his bed, he stared at the ceiling. Ever since he had been going out with Penny, he had started to believe that everyone else was as open-minded and compassionate as she was.

But obviously, that wasn't true. The incident with Andy as well as the conversation at the picnic had proved that.

For a moment, he was tempted to call Penny to talk it all over with her. But a sense of shame about his father's attitude washed over him. He couldn't admit to Penny what his own father had said about blacks. It was too humiliating.

Just forget about it, he told himself grimly. *It's only because he was around Mr. Cashman.*

And if Mr. Cashman wanted to talk like a jerk, that wasn't Neil's problem. After all, Frank Cashman was only embarrassing himself. He was a bigot, but there was nothing Neil could do about that.

However, he couldn't help wondering about his father. Was he just agreeing with Mr. Cashman to go along with a friend? Or did his father really believe what he had said?

With a groan of frustration, Neil got off the bed and started pacing back and forth across his room. At one point, he stopped at his desk, where his marine biology lab book sat open on top of a pile of homework.

One thing was clear. He couldn't invite Andy over to his house anymore. If Andy got even the smallest hint of prejudice from Mr. Free-mount, it would be the end of their friendship. And Neil definitely didn't want that to happen.

The best thing to do was wait until the whole matter faded away, Neil decided. That way, no one would get hurt.

Three

On Monday morning after homeroom, Neil grabbed his biology books from his locker and hurried down the hall to his marine biology class. He still felt embarrassed and upset about the things his father and Mr. Cashman had said, even though he didn't agree with them.

When he saw Andy, however, his mood brightened. Andy was his friend, and nothing about that had changed.

"Hey, man," he said as he sat down next to Andy.

Andy passed over the magazine he was looking at, and pointed to a cartoon. It showed the view inside a microscope, with tiny microbes looking into a microscope of their own. Neil chuckled.

"Sometimes I wonder," Andy said with a grin. "Maybe there are some giant creatures looking at us under a microscope somewhere up there."

"Yeah, maybe. I'm not sure they'd like what they see," he said, shaking his head.

"Oh, it's not so bad," Andy replied. "You just have to look on the bright side."

"You sound like you're reciting some nursery school song," Neil said, giving Andy a smile.

Andy shrugged and shook his head. "It's true."

"Hi, folks," John Archer, the marine biology teacher said. He set his grade books down on the front desk and smiled at the class. "I have a very important announcement to make before we begin."

Neil tapped his pencil on the desk to get Andy's attention, then rolled his eyes. Mr. Archer always made an announcement before they began.

"I just received a letter from the Monterey Bay Aquarium," Mr. Archer went on.

Neil saw Andy straighten up in his chair. He looked as though he were holding his breath.

"They have announced the winners of the

summer scholarship for marine biology in Monterey," Mr. Archer went on. "And I am very, very happy to say that Sweet Valley High will be sending Andy Jenkins this year."

"'All right!' Andy raised one fist in the air and then turned to give Neil a high five.

"That is excellent," Neil said. "Congratulations!"

"Congratulations, Andy," Mr. Archer said. "It's a big honor, and we're all proud of you."

Andy was smiling broadly. "Thanks a lot, Mr. Archer. I really wanted it." The students near Andy all called out their congratulations.

Neil tapped Andy on the head with his pencil. "Don't get conceited or anything," he said. "But let's celebrate after school, OK?"

"Sure thing," Andy replied with a laugh. "How about the Dairi Burger? And I want Tracy to come. She'll be so psyched. Bring Penny, too."

"It's a deal," Neil said.

In Neil's opinion, nobody deserved that scholarship more than Andy. He worked harder than anyone in their marine biology class and was always doing extra-credit assignments. It was only right that Andy should have the chance to study at the famous aquarium.

Then, remembering what had happened Friday, Neil felt a twinge of worry. He hoped nothing would happen to spoil Andy's triumph.

Elizabeth carried her tray to her usual table in the cafeteria. She saw at once that all of her friends were reading *The Oracle.*

"Hi," she said to her best friend, Enid Rollins.

Her curly brown hair bounced around her face as she turned to smile at Elizabeth. "What kind of a riot were you planning to start with this survey?" she teased.

"I don't get it," Elizabeth protested, sitting down between her boyfriend, Todd Wilkins, and Enid. "I thought it was just a harmless little question."

"I'll tell you what I'd change," Manuel Lopez spoke up. "I'd change the way they teach history around here. This whole area of California was settled by the Spanish from Mexico for centuries before white Americans came over the Rockies. The Spanish were the real discoverers of California."

Manuel's girlfriend, Sandra Bacon, looked surprised. "I didn't realize that," she said.

"That's what I mean," Manuel said. "That's the whole problem. A lot of teachers tend to skip over that part of California's history."

"We used to go on field trips to the old Spanish missions when we were in elementary school," Ken Matthews put in.

Manuel just rolled his eyes.

"Whoa!" Jade Wu said. "Doesn't anyone care about the *real* issues?" Her brown eyes were twinkling mischievously. "Like maybe getting rid of this boring cafeteria food and putting in a couple of pizza ovens?"

Everyone laughed but Manuel.

"Listen," Dana Larson, the lead singer of The Droids, said, waving her hand. "This is what I'd change—pay less attention to boys' sports. It's totally ridiculous that the whole school focuses on these primitive macho competitions."

Aaron Dallas, Dana's boyfriend, stared at her. "So when I play soccer, that's primitive macho competition? And here I thought it was just soccer."

"Boys' sports programs get more money than girls' sports," Sandra put in. "I read it in the school budget outline when it was up for a vote."

"Boys' sports use more equipment," Todd Wilkins said. "It makes sense that they need more money."

Dana shook her head. "It doesn't make sense that they put boys' sports on the front page of the paper and girls' on the back," she pointed out.

"Who cares about field hockey?" John Pfeifer joked.

The conversation spun around the table, growing louder and more heated. Elizabeth looked at Enid and shook her head. Apparently, there were more resentments and complaints about Sweet Valley High than she realized. Taking a look around the familiar cafeteria, she suddenly wondered how well she really knew her school.

"You guys get a booth, I'll get some sodas," Neil said as he, Andy, Tracy, and Penny walked into the Dairi Burger. They had driven over in two cars because Tracy had to leave soon to go to her job at a toy store in the mall.

Several people called out congratulations to Andy, but he looked embarrassed and shrugged it off. "Cokes and diet Cokes," he said to Neil, then turned to find a booth.

"I'll get us some burgers, too," Neil offered. "I'm starving."

Once he had a tray full of sodas and hamburgers, he wove his way through the maze of tables to the booth where Andy and the two girls were sitting.

"In honor of brilliant scientists everywhere," Neil toasted, raising his soda cup.

"Here, here," Penny joined in.

"I've been to that aquarium," Tracy said. The pretty, slender black girl smiled at her boyfriend. "They have a huge tank for sea otters. They are so adorable."

Andy rolled his eyes. "You think everything's adorable, even abalones."

"Well, they are kind of cute, too." Tracy laughed. "Adorable abalones."

Penny took a swallow of her soda. "I bet you can't say that ten times fast."

Instantly, Andy and Tracy both tried it, but they got hopelessly tongue-tied, and the whole group burst into laughter. Their joking banter continued for the next half hour.

After they had finished eating, Tracy turned to the others. "I hate to say it, but I have to go."

Penny looked at her watch and nodded. "I guess we should get going, too."

Tracy stood up. "I'll meet you in the parking lot. I just want to stop by and talk to Jade Wu for a second."

Penny went to the counter to order a soda to

take with her, while Neil and Andy, joking and kidding around, strolled outside.

"Hey, Jenkins."

Neil and Andy both stopped. Charlie Cashman, Jerry McAllister, Jim Sturbridge, and Ron Reese were all leaning against Charlie's beat-up blue Camaro. Jerry, also known as Crunch, a dropout from Sweet Valley High, spent a lot of time with Charlie. Jim Sturbridge and Ron Reese, both seniors at the school, belonged to a rough crowd. Warning bells went off in Neil's head when he saw the group and heard the dangerous tone in Charlie's voice.

"Let's just go," Neil said under his breath to Andy.

"You got it,' Andy agreed. They started to walk past the Camaro.

Charlie pushed himself off the car and stepped right in front of Andy.

There was a moment of tense silence, and Neil could feel his heart pounding in his chest.

"What's up, Cashman?" Andy said pleasantly, but the look in his eyes was anything but friendly.

Charlie glanced back at his friends, then looked at Andy and sneered. "I heard you got picked out for a special prize because you're black."

Andy's jaw muscles tensed. "I heard it was because I earned it," he said stiffly.

"No way," Charlie scoffed. "It's that bogus affirmative action—you guys taking away from us, just because you want special privileges."

"Shut up, Charlie," Neil said. Charlie really did sound exactly like his father.

Charlie's gaze flicked to Neil and then back to Andy. "Don't you expect to get special treatment because you're disadvantaged?" he asked scornfully.

"Not from you," Andy shot back. He stepped to the side and walked away.

Charlie looked at Neil. "He sure acts conceited for a black guy."

"Just shut up," Neil repeated. He was feeling angrier—and more nervous—every second. Shooting Charlie an icy glare, Neil ran to catch up with Andy. The mocking laughter of the group followed him.

"Hey," Neil said, falling into step beside his friend. "Don't let him get to you."

Andy was staring straight ahead, and his jaw was still tightly clenched. He looked as if he was having to fight to keep his temper under control.

"Look," Neil went on, casting an uneasy glance back at the other boys. "This guy's

31

father is a real jerk, I know. And besides, he's having a bad time at work. Maybe he's taking it out at home. That's where Charlie gets it from."

In his head, Neil could hear Frank Cashman complaining about the "stupid affirmative action" at Patman Canning. He had probably been griping about it at home, too.

Andy took a few deep breaths and let them out slowly.

"I don't want to cause any trouble," he said in a low voice, "but I don't see why I have to be insulted just because *his* father is in a bad mood."

"I know, I know," Neil said. He looked over his shoulder again and saw that Penny and Tracy were coming out of the Dairi Burger together. "Here come—"

"Don't tell Tracy," Andy said abruptly. "She'll get upset." He looked Neil in the eyes. "And don't tell Penny, either."

Neil couldn't believe Andy still wanted to keep the whole thing to himself. "But, Andy, there could be real trouble—"

"Just let me handle it my own way," Andy said in a frustrated tone.

Neil swallowed hard. Charlie and the others

were watching Tracy silently, so far. Neil just hoped they had had enough for one day.

"OK. If you say so," he agreed.

"Wait up, guys!" Tracy called.

Neil watched Andy try to put an unconcerned expression on his face as the two girls joined them.

"I'll walk you to your car," Andy said to Tracy.

Tracy gave Penny a surprised smile. "This guy has manners, doesn't he?"

Neil suspected Andy was worried about Charlie still being in the parking lot. Neil was worried, too. He watched them walk to Tracy's car.

"Are you OK?" Penny asked suddenly.

Neil glanced at her and then looked away. "Sure."

"Oh, no!" Tracy's voice reached them.

Neil broke into a run. When he reached Andy and Tracy, they were walking around her car, examining the tires. All four of them were flat. And Neil had an awful feeling he knew who was responsible.

Four

"What am I going to do?" Tracy wailed. "I don't *believe* this!"

"I believe it," Andy said angrily.

He glanced swiftly across the parking lot as the blue Camaro pulled out, tires squealing. It sounded almost like mocking laughter.

Tracy's hands flew to her cheeks. "This is terrible," she said. "I'm going to be so late for work."

"I can drive you over," Neil offered. "Don't worry about your car. We'll take care of it."

He felt sick inside. There was absolutely no question in his mind that Charlie Cashman was responsible and that Tracy's tires were flat for no other reason than because she was black. Obviously, Charlie thought that was enough of a reason to vandalize her car. It made Neil furious.

"What happened?" Penny asked as she walked over to join them. She looked at their stricken faces and then noticed the tires. "Oh, no! How . . . ?"

"That jerk—" Andy cut himself off. "First my locker, now this. Next time I see Cashman—"

"You don't know for sure Charlie trashed your locker," Neil put in anxiously. He felt just as outraged as Andy. But, even though he was pretty certain that Charlie had had something to do with it, it might have been one of his friends, and not Charlie himself.

Furious, Andy turned on Neil. "Oh, no? Who do you think did it? Tracy?"

"No, of course not." Neil shook his head. The whole situation was getting out of control. "All I meant was—"

"I know what you meant," Andy broke in. "Don't go around accusing people without any proof, right?" He snapped at Neil. "Sorry, but Charlie didn't exactly sign his name. Maybe he will next time."

Neil didn't know what to say.

Andy kicked one of the tires and dug his

hands into his pockets. "Darn," he muttered under his breath.

Neil gave Penny an imploring look, but she appeared just as uncomfortable as he felt. Neil tried again. "Andy, let's just—"

Tracy let out a sigh. "Listen, you guys. I really have to get going—" She sounded very upset.

"Sorry," Andy said gruffly.

Neil swallowed hard. "Come on. I'll take you to work."

"Yeah." Andy nodded. "I'll call a tow truck and wait for it to come, Tracy. Don't worry about it. I'll get your car fixed."

"Do you want me to stay with you?" Penny asked Andy.

He shook his head. "No. I can handle it by myself."

"OK," she said, "If you're sure."

"I'm sure."

Neil gave his friend one last look. He felt terrible about leaving Andy there alone to fix Tracy's car, but he knew the best way to help was to take Tracy to work. Groaning to himself, he said good-bye, then headed back across the parking lot with Tracy and Penny.

In just a matter of days, life had suddenly

become more complicated than he had ever anticipated.

Before homeroom Tuesday morning, Neil saw Andy walking across the front lawn toward school.

"Andy! Wait up!" he yelled. Neil ran to catch up with him.

Andy turned and stopped, but he didn't say anything. He gave Neil a preoccupied nod instead of a hello.

"Did you get everything straightened out yesterday?" Neil asked.

"Yes," Andy replied curtly, as they continued walking toward the front school steps. It was clear that he was still simmering. "I paid forty-five bucks for a tow to the tire center. Then I had to bum a ride home, borrow money from my mother, and get back to the tire center. By then it was five o'clock, and they told me they couldn't get the job done until this morning. So I guess you could say it's all straightened out."

Neil felt terrible. Even though it wasn't his responsibility, he thought of offering to help pay. But something held him back. He suspected that Andy wouldn't accept the offer in the spirit it was intended.

Something else was worrying Neil, too. He was pretty sure Andy was angry enough now to confront Charlie. There was no telling what would happen in that situation. If Charlie's buddies were with him—and they almost always were—Andy would be outnumbered four to one. Considering how angry Andy was, Neil was afraid the confrontation might get violent.

"Listen," Neil began hesitantly. "Try not to let it get to you." He groped for the right words but couldn't find them. "Think—think of how Martin Luther King, Jr., would react to a situation like this—"

"Who do you think you are?" Andy gasped. "Don't talk to *me* about Dr. King!"

Stung, Neil stared at Andy. A blush of embarrassment washed over his cheeks. "Sorry," he mumbled. "I was just trying to—"

"I know what you were trying to do," Andy said, quickening his stride.

"Andy!" Feeling hurt and confused, Neil stopped on the steps. He knew what a hard time his friend must be going through, but he couldn't seem to find the right way to show his sympathy. Somehow he had to get through to Andy.

Andy slowed to a halt at the front door.

"Listen," Neil went on when Andy finally turned to look at him. "I think this thing could get way out of hand if you don't do something about it now. You should tell Mr. Cooper—or—or one of the teachers you like, like Mr. Collins or Mr. Archer . . ." Seeing the stubborn look in Andy's eyes, Neil's voice trailed off.

"You think I should go to a teacher?" Andy asked in a bitter voice. "Want to hear a good story? This same sort of thing happened in junior high, before I moved here. And the teacher I went to said, 'Just ignore it, Andy. Don't make trouble.' That's the kind of help I got. I'm not asking again."

Neil gestured vaguely. He knew he wasn't being any help at all. "But that wouldn't happen here."

"Oh, so Sweet Valley is special?" Andy asked sarcastically. He jabbed a finger at Neil. "Look. I can handle it on my own. I don't need help from anyone, especially from any *white* person."

Neil felt a heavy thump in his chest, almost like a punch. He was completely taken aback, speechless.

The look in Andy's eyes was dark and brooding. Without a word, he went into the school. The door slammed in Neil's face.

*　　*　　*

There was an assembly that morning, so Neil didn't see Andy in marine biology class. In fact, Neil hardly glimpsed him again all day. Once, before lunchtime, he saw Andy at the far end of the hallway. But by the time Neil got there, Andy had rounded the corner and was gone. Neil didn't like to consider the possibility that Andy was avoiding him, but it seemed that was exactly what was happening.

But why? It was almost as if Andy held a grudge against every single student at Sweet Valley High because of Charlie's bigotry. It was true that many of them hadn't ever faced real hardships or discrimination, but that didn't make them terrible people. And it didn't mean they wouldn't understand or stick up for Andy, either. Neil was pretty sure just about everyone would be totally outraged by what Charlie had done—if they knew. But Andy didn't want them to know, and that was something else Neil didn't understand.

A couple of kids who had been at the Dairi Burger came up to him and asked about what had happened. Neil had played the whole thing down. He didn't like doing it, but that was what Andy wanted.

Now, at the end of the day, Neil felt as if he might explode if he didn't talk about what was going on. He closed his locker and headed for the *Oracle* office. He had to find Penny.

When he looked into the newspaper office, Penny was there with Elizabeth Wakefield. No one else was around. Neil breathed a sigh of relief. Elizabeth was a friend, and just as good a listener as Penny was. He shut the door behind him and sat down at the conference table.

"Hi, Neil," Elizabeth said, giving him a friendly smile.

"Hi," he said, slumping in his chair. He didn't know how to begin. The thoughts that were chasing each other through his head made him feel so confused.

Penny looked at him questioningly. "How's Andy today?" she asked, getting right to the heart of the matter as usual.

Neil shrugged. "He's really mad," he said. Then, glancing at Elizabeth, he explained, "Charlie Cashman and his buddies have been pulling these racist stunts against Andy and Tracy lately."

Elizabeth's eyes widened. "I don't believe it," she said.

"You don't?" Penny asked in a dry tone.

41

Elizabeth shook her head. "No. I mean, I believe you, I just never thought something like that could happen here."

"Me, neither," Neil agreed. "But it's true. It's so petty—it's just because Andy's black. That's the only reason."

Elizabeth looked horrified. "When did all this start? What's Charlie been doing?"

As Penny filled Elizabeth in on what had happened, Neil stared at his hands and tried to sort out his feelings.

What bothered him the most was that Andy's reaction was so much like Charlie's: Andy had insisted he didn't need any help from white people—*any* white people, regardless of what they were like. That was the worst thing. It appeared that Andy saw the situation as white versus black, just the way Charlie did. Neil wanted to be there for his friend, but he had to admit he found Andy's attitude frustrating.

"Has Andy reported any of this to Mr. Cooper?" Elizabeth asked, breaking into Neil's thoughts.

Neil shook his head irritably. "No—that's what's so frustrating. He says he can handle it on his own. He says he's not asking for any help from anyone *white*. Period."

There was a stunned silence in the small office. Penny and Elizabeth stared at Neil.

"He said that?" Penny asked. An anxious frown creased her forehead. She began tapping her pencil nervously on the desk.

"Yes." Neil raked one hand back through his hair. "That's what I don't get—I mean, that's racism, too, isn't it? Making generalizations about a race like that?"

Elizabeth leaned forward on her elbows. "I don't know if that's exactly the same thing," she said. "It *is* true that white people have discriminated against blacks for hundreds of years. Maybe Andy has a good reason to feel angry and suspicious about the white establishment."

"That's true," Penny agreed.

Neil bit his lip. "Yeah, but he said that to *me*. I mean, we're supposed to be friends. How can he put me in that category with—"

"Just go easy on him," Penny advised. "He needs support right now, and a friend. Don't judge him while he's upset. That's not fair."

"You're right," Neil said. "I do want to help him. But the question is, will he let me?"

Five

When Elizabeth got home that afternoon, she went straight to her room. She needed to think. It greatly disturbed her to know what was going on between Andy Jenkins and Charlie Cashman. She had always thought of Sweet Valley High as such a warm, friendly school, where people got along fairly well with one another. There had always been small problems, of course, but they were nothing compared to this.

"Hi, Liz," Jessica said, strolling into Elizabeth's room. Then, seeing her sister's sober expression, she asked, "What's wrong with you?"

"I don't know," Elizabeth said slowly. She was sitting on her bed. "Did you ever have that weird feeling when you realize things aren't the way you thought they were?"

Jessica rolled her eyes dramatically. "Tell me about it. Like when you are one-hundred-percent positive a guy really likes you, and then you find out he really likes someone else."

"Well . . ." Elizabeth made a skeptical face. "That's not exactly what I meant." She pulled a pillow into her lap and frowned. She loved Jessica, but she wasn't sure Jessica was the most sensitive person in the world when it came to some subjects. "Do you think people at school are pretty open-minded? I mean, accepting of things?"

"Sure," Jessica replied easily. She stood in front of Elizabeth's full-length mirror and examined her eyes. "Everyone is basically cool."

Elizabeth looked at her sister. Jessica always seemed to be so carefree.

But life wasn't carefree for a lot of people. Elizabeth thought over some of the surprising reactions she had gotten to her survey in *The Oracle*. It had only been a day since the paper came out, and already she had received over a dozen responses. She had to admit, she had never seen any real problems at school before. But now she was seeing them everywhere.

"Don't you sometimes feel like some people get more privileges than other people, just because of who they are?" she asked her sister.

Jessica nodded. "Oh, well, sure. Lila, for one, the spoiled brat. And Bruce Patman—he thinks he's king of California."

"And people pretty much let him get away with it, too," Elizabeth said, still frowning. "Why do they?"

"Who knows?" Jessica shrugged and then flopped down beside Elizabeth on her bed. "Some people just seem to have more in this world, I guess."

Elizabeth arched her eyebrows. "People like Bruce Patman?"

"Well, sure. He's rich," Jessica said. "And even though I don't like him very much, I still have to admit he's gorgeous."

"So in other words, people who are good-looking and rich get extra, is that what you're saying?" Elizabeth demanded hotly.

"I know, it's not fair," Jessica said. "But, hey, I don't make the rules."

Elizabeth stood up, threw the pillow on the bed, and began to pace. "Then I want to talk to the person who made the rules," she said fiercely. "We need some new ones."

"What are you complaining for?" Jessica laughed. "I notice you fit into the lucky category. We're not stinking rich, but we're OK."

"Jessica!" Elizabeth whirled around to face her twin. "Didn't it ever occur to you that if we're fortunate, that means we have a responsibility to make sure other people are treated fairly?"

Jessica looked taken aback. "What got into you all of a sudden?"

Elizabeth sank into the chair at her desk. "I've got news for you, Jess. Things at Sweet Valley are not as great as you think." Elizabeth told her twin about Andy's locker and the incident at the Dairi Burger.

"Charlie Cashman's always been a total jerk," Jessica said when Elizabeth had finished. "If you ask me, Andy should just ignore him completely."

Elizabeth sighed. Jessica had a good heart, but she wasn't always the most understanding person when it came to other people's problems. Ignoring Charlie wasn't going to make him stop making racial attacks against Andy. Elizabeth just hoped something, or someone, *would* stop him, before something else happened.

Neil slammed his math book shut and sat brooding at the desk in his bedroom. The more he thought about it, the more indignant he felt about the way Andy was treating him. How could Andy only see him as a stereotypical white person? It was pretty clear that that was how he felt. Now that racial problems had come up, Andy just assumed that Neil was like every other white person—and that meant being against blacks. It wasn't fair. Neil knew he didn't deserve to be treated that way, and he felt really hurt that Andy had that knee-jerk reaction.

"Neil! Dinner's ready!" Mrs. Freemount called.

Neil jumped up, glad to have something else to think about. As he ran down the stairs, he heard his father's voice.

"What a scene at work today," Mr. Freemount said.

"What happened, Paul?" Mrs. Freemount asked. She put a casserole dish on the dining table and smiled at Neil as he sat down.

Mr. Freemount loosened his tie. "Poor Frank,

he's really getting it from Willis now. I think Willis is deliberately provoking him, trying to get him steamed up."

"What did Mr. Cashman do, Dad?" Neil asked.

"Nothing. Absolutely nothing," his father stated emphatically.

Carol Freemount looked doubtful. "There must have been something."

"I'm telling you, it was nothing," Mr. Freemount insisted. "Willis is out to prove something because he's a black man with white guys under him. That's the only reason he's picking on Frank." He jabbed at the casserole with a serving spoon.

Neil watched his father closely. He couldn't tell for sure if Mr. Willis really was being hard on Mr. Cashman or if his father was blowing the whole thing out of proportion just because Mr. Willis was black. It really hurt to think that he couldn't always count on his father to be fair.

Mr. Freemount noticed Neil's steady gaze and flushed red.

"What?" he said defensively. "You think I'm exaggerating, right? I guess you're on Willis's side."

"I don't even know the guy," Neil mumbled, looking away. "I'm not on anyone's side."

He thought of Andy and winced, aware of the irony of his words. A few days earlier he would have said without question that he was on Andy's side. But Andy didn't want him on his side. A fresh wave of hurt and anger spread through him, and Neil suppressed a sigh.

So much for being friends, he thought glumly.

They ate dinner in silence. Mr. Freemount was in a terrible mood about the situation at work, and Neil was too preoccupied to make conversation with his mother. As they were clearing the table, Neil heard a car pull into the driveway and honk.

"Neil, does one of your friends have a blue Camaro?" Mrs. Freemount asked as she looked out the window.

Neil glanced outside. He felt a dull thud in the pit of his stomach when he saw who it was. "It's Charlie," he said slowly. He hesitated for a moment and then went out to the front hall to open the door.

"Hi, Charlie," he said warily. *What is he doing here?* he wondered.

Charlie stopped on the top step. "Hey, Neil." He sounded nervous. "I was just—you know— driving around, so I thought I'd stop by."

"Charlie?" Mrs. Freemount called, stepping into the doorway behind Neil. "Hi. Come on in."

Charlie shook his head. "No, thanks, Mrs. Freemount. I just stopped by to say hi."

Neil was thrown off balance. Charlie wasn't the type who "just stopped by to say hi." He looked shaken up and didn't seem at all like his usual, arrogant self. When his mother was out of earshot, Neil asked, "What's up?"

"Nothing much. I just had to get out of the house. My dad's having a fit over work . . ." He shrugged.

"Yeah, my dad's acting pretty foul, too," Neil said.

He noticed the tired look on Charlie's face and realized that things were probably pretty bad at the Cashmans'. Knowing Mr. Cashman, Neil guessed it must be very unpleasant over there. Charlie was the last person Neil wanted to see at the moment, but Charlie was obviously really upset, or he wouldn't have come over. He must have figured Neil would know what was going on and that he wouldn't have to explain.

"Want to cruise around for a while?" Charlie asked after a moment.

Neil hesitated. Charlie was a total jerk, but

right now he looked so troubled and . . . needy. Neil didn't have the heart to make him feel worse. "Sure. Why not," he said with a shrug. He felt sorry for Charlie. After all, it wasn't Charlie's fault that Mr. Cashman was such a jerk.

Neil ducked back inside the house. "Mom! I'm going out with Charlie. I'll be back soon." Turning to Charlie, he said, "OK. Let's go."

"All right," Charlie said, smiling. "Let's hit the road."

Neil didn't say anything as he got into the Camaro and slammed the car door shut.

"Pick a tape or something," Charlie offered, pointing to the backseat with his thumb. "There's a bunch of cassettes."

While Neil sorted through the loose tapes, Charlie turned the Camaro down the street and stepped on the gas. Neil just barely stopped himself from toppling into the backseat.

"Whoa!" he called out. "This car really moves."

"No kidding," Charlie agreed. "Let's get out on the highway, then you'll really see her in action."

Neil put a Rolling Stones tape into the cassette deck and turned the volume up. Deafening music pounded through the car. Maybe this wouldn't be so bad after all, he thought, tapping his foot to the beat.

"All right!" Charlie yelled, giving Neil a thumbs-up sign.

The Camaro swerved around a corner and onto the highway. Neil glanced at Charlie. He knew he should say something about all the cruel stunts Charlie had been pulling on Andy. But then again, Andy *had* told him to butt out of it. And besides, Neil didn't know if he wanted to get into a big confrontation with Charlie right now. This was the first time that he had ever seen Charlie in a sympathetic light. Why should he go out of his way to ruin that? Maybe it was a sign that Charlie was changing.

Neil decided the best thing to do was just sit back and try to enjoy the ride. They raced down the highway for ten miles and then pulled off into a residential neighborhood.

"Guess who lives out here?" Charlie asked. He moved his eyebrows up and down, like Groucho Marx.

Neil laughed. "Who?"

"Chrome Dome Cooper, our beloved principal, that's who." Charlie was watching the houses as they drove down the street. "Right . . . here."

Charlie stopped the car in front of a small

brick house. Several lights were on downstairs. Neil felt a prickle of anticipation. "What are you going to do?" he asked nervously.

"Just say hello," Charlie said innocently. Then he put his hand down on the horn for ten full seconds. The front porch light went on.

"Come on," Neil said. "Let's get out of here."

Charlie let out a wolf howl and then stomped on the gas pedal. The Camaro shot away, tires squealing.

"You're crazy," Neil said, frowning.

"I am what I am and that's all that I am," Charlie replied in a Popeye voice.

Neil shook his head. Charlie was pretty wild, and he did some outrageous things. But Neil supposed it wasn't completely his fault. The guy had a lot of rotten stuff to deal with at home, and he needed an outlet for it. If Mr. Cashman was in danger of losing his job, he was probably taking it out on Charlie and Mrs. Cashman more than usual. Neil could understand why Charlie was getting out of control. Not that that excused the awful way Charlie had been treating Andy—it didn't.

After an hour, Neil was completely bored of honking in front of people's houses and racing around. His thoughts went back to his math homework. He still had ten problems to do.

"Hey, look," he said. "I really have to get home soon."

Charlie nodded. "No problem. Next time let's make a little trouble."

Neil scowled. "Yeah, well . . ."

He didn't say anything more. When they pulled into the Freemounts' driveway, he gave Charlie a brief wave. "See you in school tomorrow," he said.

"Right." Charlie put the Camaro into reverse and backed out into the street without looking. Then he raced away again.

Neil stood on the front steps, listening to the sound of the Camaro's engine fade into the distance. Suddenly he felt drained.

"What was I doing?" he asked himself out loud. "I must be losing my mind."

Suddenly he couldn't believe that he had just spent time hanging out with Charlie Cashman. Charlie was the very reason his friendship with Andy was on such shaky ground. Andy was Neil's friend, not Charlie. A tremendous weight of guilt settled over Neil.

He didn't want to think about how Andy would feel if he knew. Ashamed, Neil hurried inside and went up to his bedroom.

Six

Neil leaned against his car after school on Wednesday as he waited for Andy. He was still feeling upset about the ride he had taken with Charlie the night before. After he had returned home, he had done a lot of thinking. He hadn't enjoyed the ride, but he shouldn't have gone out with Charlie at all—not after what Charlie had done to Andy. Neil had made an extra effort to be nice to Andy during the day, and Andy seemed to be warming up to him. At least they were still friends enough for Neil to give Andy a lift home.

"Hey, Freemount!" came a familiar voice. "What's up, man?"

Neil glanced up, a sinking feeling in the pit of his stomach. Charlie was walking toward him with Ron Reese and Jim Sturbridge. Neil wished he could vanish into thin air. He looked around anxiously, but there was no way to avoid them.

"We're going up to Secca Lake to do a little partying," Charlie went on as he walked up.

The three boys surrounded Neil. He stayed where he was, leaning casually against his car. He hoped he didn't look as tense and jumpy as he felt.

"Sorry," he said. "I'm waiting for somebody I promised to drive home."

"That wouldn't be your black buddy, would it?" Charlie sneered. "What are you wasting your time on him for, anyway?"

Neil gritted his teeth and looked Charlie squarely in the eye. "He's a friend, like I said. So just lay off him, OK?"

"Ooooh!" Charlie said, pretending to be offended.

Neil felt his stomach turn. "I'm not going with you," he said in a tightly controlled voice. "So why don't you guys just go on, all right?"

Charlie looked at the others and shook his head sadly. "Poor Neil. He has to stick up for his black buddy. There's your affirmative action, again."

"Jeez, Charlie!" Neil blurted out, glaring at him. "Just get lost, will you?" He pushed his way past the three boys and started to head back toward the school.

Then he saw Andy walking toward him. Andy stopped when he saw Neil with Charlie and the others. A look of distrust was on his face. Holding back an angry curse, Neil broke into a jog to meet up with his friend.

"Hey, Andy," he said.

Andy stood where he was. "Now you're friends with Cashman?" he asked stonily.

"No, no way," Neil insisted. He pushed his hair back. "They were giving me a hard time about you, but I was sticking up for you. I was."

Andy laughed sarcastically. "Oh, gee, Neil. Thank you so much! I really appreciate being defended by you." He grimaced and looked away.

"What's wrong with you?" Neil asked. He stepped in front of Andy, but his friend wouldn't look at him. "Andy, we're supposed to be buddies, remember? I do stuff for you, you do stuff for me, that's the way it works. I'd stick up for any of my friends if someone was trashing them."

"Except that none of your friends get trashed except me," Andy said. "Because I'm your *black* friend."

"Oh, come on, Andy!" Neil began in a frustrated tone. "What does that—"

"Look," Andy cut in, "you can't say you're my friend and also be Cashman's friend at the same time."

Neil was breathing hard. Hadn't Andy heard a word he'd said? He didn't consider Charlie his friend. He didn't even like the guy. He felt completely exasperated that Andy was putting him on the defensive this way. Before he knew it, he blurted out, "Hey, I'll be friends with anyone I want, OK? I don't need your permission. I've known Charlie for a long time, and if I feel like hanging out with him, I will."

"Suit yourself," Andy said.

"Andy—"

Just then, Tracy drove up and rolled down her window. "Hi, guys," she said cheerfully. "Want me to drop you off at home on my way to work, Andy?"

Neil and Andy glared at each other for a moment. Then Andy nodded. "Sure." Without another word to Neil, Andy got into Tracy's car. Tracy waved as they drove off, and Neil stared after them. He realized he was shaking. He didn't know whom he was mad at the most—Charlie, Andy, or himself.

Gradually, Neil shook himself out of the daze he was in. Taking a deep breath to steady himself, he turned to walk back to his car.

Charlie and the others were still there, watching him with amused expressions.

"Gee, I guess you guys are really best friends, huh?" Charlie said, a sarcastic smirk on his face. "Really tight."

Ron Reese and Jim Sturbridge chuckled.

"Just drop it," Neil said. He reached for the car door handle.

"Listen, Neil," Charlie said, cutting in front of him. The smile was gone from his face. "I'm telling you, black and white just don't mix. Can't you see that? Stick with your own kind. You'll be better off."

Neil waited in stubborn silence until Charlie was through and then calmly opened his car door. Without looking at the other boys, he slammed the door shut. Then he drove off.

Penny shut the filing cabinet drawer and stared off into space. The *Oracle* office was quiet. Everyone had left except for her. Usually, she liked to be alone in the newspaper office. But today she felt uneasy and nervous. She wished there was someone else to talk to.

Deep in thought, she sat down at the conference table where Elizabeth had been working that afternoon. A neat pile of papers was stacked to one side of a typewriter. Glancing at them, Penny saw that they were answers to the survey in the school paper. She picked one up to read.

> I don't think it's fair that the Pi Beta Alpha sorority girls get to head all the dance committees and prom committees. I don't think there should be any kind of club that gets to keep people out because of how they dress or if they have a boyfriend.

"I agree," Penny said aloud. Frowning, she picked up another one. The next response read:

> It's not right that girls aren't considered good enough to play varsity football. If you've got the speed and the skill, there's no reason a girl couldn't be a quarterback.

Penny grinned. She tried to think who could have written that. There were plenty of great athletes on the girls' teams. But from the sound of it, there was one who wanted to play football.

She jotted a note in the margin for Elizabeth. "See if you can figure out who this is. Maybe it's a good item for the 'Eyes and Ears' column." Elizabeth wrote the popular gossip column for the paper. An item about a girl who wanted to try out for the football team would certainly raise some eyebrows around Sweet Valley High.

Still smiling, she pulled another answer from the pile.

> I think they should kick out anyone from this school who isn't a real American. Like blacks, Hispanics, and Asians. They always get advantages over us.

A wave of heat flashed across Penny's face. She reread the response, feeling sick with anger.

In her mind, she saw a picture of a typical Sweet Valley High crowd. Everyone was always living life to the fullest, getting caught up in dreams and disappointments. Everyone was so *normal*. How could there be such hatred just under the surface?

Penny shivered slightly and folded her arms across her chest.

I should never have let Elizabeth do this, she thought.

But she knew it would have been wrong *not* to have the survey. If there were hidden feelings like that at Sweet Valley High, they had to be brought out into the open. Keeping them in the dark, ignoring them, would only make things worse. *Look at what's happening to Andy*, she thought. Keeping everything a secret didn't seem to be helping any, from what she could tell, and it was putting a strain on his friendship with Neil. Somehow, the prejudice had to be exposed. That was the only way to get rid of it. And even then, it would probably be painful for everyone.

Her eyes were drawn back to the sheet in her hand. Shaking her head, she slowly crushed it into a ball in her fist.

"Neil! Telephone!"

Neil had been lying on his bed in the dark since dinnertime. For a moment, he contemplated pretending to be asleep.

"Neil! It's Penny!"

Sighing, Neil sat up and switched on his bedside lamp. He ran one hand through his hair and then got up to get the extension in the hallway.

"Hello?" he said.

"Neil? It's me," Penny said. "Are you all right? You sound sick or something."

"No, I'm fine," Neil said half-heartedly. "What's up?"

"Nothing, I guess," Penny went on. "I just wanted to know how everything is. You know— with Andy and all. We didn't get a chance to talk very much today."

Neil stared at his fingernails, hesitating for a moment. He wanted to tell Penny what he was thinking and feeling. But the truth was, he wasn't sure himself. It seemed that whatever he did was the wrong thing, and he was starting to get fed up—with Charlie Cashman *and* with Andy. He wanted to be more understanding of Andy, but he was beginning to wonder if that was possible anymore. But would Penny understand that?

"It's OK," he said in a guarded tone. "Nothing's different."

"Does that mean—is Charlie still being—" Penny broke off uncertainly.

Neil shrugged. "Charlie is still Charlie, if that's what you mean. But I have a feeling he's going to get even worse."

"Why?" Penny asked.

"I just heard from my father," Neil began.

He glanced over his shoulder and lowered his voice. "Charlie's dad got fired today from his job. By the black foreman at Patman Canning."

Penny got the point instantly. "Oh, no. So Charlie is probably going to take it out—"

"On Andy," Neil supplied. "Right."

"Neil," Penny spoke up. There was an urgent tone in her voice. "Neil, something's going to happen. I feel like something terrible's been going on underground for a long time, and it's about to come out in the open. I mean, I can't even believe what's really going on around here—in people's heads."

"I know," Neil said softly.

"Andy really needs you now," Penny went on.

"Right," Neil said evasively. If Andy needed him so badly, he sure had a funny way of showing it. He suddenly had the awful feeling he was going to cry. "Listen, my mom's calling me," he lied. "I'll talk to you tomorrow, all right?"

"OK," Penny said. "Bye."

Neil hung up the phone and then stared at it. "I don't know what to think anymore," he said softly to himself. "And I don't know what to do."

Seven

There was a marine biology quiz on Friday. Neil got to class early and skimmed through his notes one last time. When Andy sat down next to him, Neil glanced up.

"Hi," he said, smiling hesitantly.

Andy nodded. "What's up?"

"Not much," Neil said. He looked at Andy again, hoping to see some sign that things were still the same between them. But Andy was scowling at his lab notebook, concentrating on last-minute studying.

"Ready for this quiz?" Neil went on casually.

"I guess so," Andy replied. He gave Neil a polite smile. "How about you?"

"Sure," Neil said. He flipped through a few more pages in his notebook, trying to act unconcerned. Just a few weeks ago, they would have been bantering and joking, getting along great. Now they were being polite but reserved, like strangers. It felt so phony and unnatural that Neil wanted to scream or break something.

"Books on the floor, please," Mr. Archer said as he began passing out the quiz. "The experiment setup for questions five through seven is on the lab desk at the back of the room. No talking, please."

Neil gave Andy another questioning glance, but Andy wouldn't meet his eyes.

Gritting his teeth, Neil ripped a sheet of paper from his notebook and forced himself to think about the quiz. But no matter how hard he tried, he couldn't stop thinking about how messed up everything was.

This is crazy, he stormed inwardly. *What am I trying so hard for? Nothing is worth this much trouble.*

He blinked suddenly, realizing he was staring out the window instead of working on the quiz. Neil felt another flash of resentment toward Andy.

I'll probably flunk this quiz. He knew he had to stop dwelling on the problem and pay attention to his work. But it was almost impossible to stop obsessing about Andy and Charlie and his father and Mr. Willis and Mr. Cashman and the whole mess.

Letting out a sigh, he stood up to look at the experiment in the back of the room. He recognized what the setup was for, but he couldn't remember what chemical reaction was supposed to take place. He sat down again, tapped his pencil on the desk, and fumed.

Gradually, he was able to put the situation out of his mind and concentrate on the quiz. But he knew he wasn't giving it all his attention. As Mr. Archer picked up the papers, Neil slumped in his chair.

"Oh, man," he muttered. "What a joke."

Andy picked his books up off the floor. "It wasn't that hard," he said.

"Yeah, well . . ." Neil sighed again, and when Andy looked at him, he managed a faint smile. "Next time."

"Right," Andy said.

When class was over, Neil still felt terrible. He knew Andy was probably feeling just as awful about the state of their friendship. At least, he assumed so. Neil thought about Penny and what she would suggest. She had said on the phone Wednesday night that Andy really needed his support. The guy *was* his friend. Even if Andy was acting weird to him, Neil knew Andy was the real victim, not him. He should give it another try.

"Do you have band practice today?" Neil asked Andy as they headed for the door. It felt totally fake to be making conversation that way, but he didn't know what else to do.

"No," Andy said, stepping into the crowded hallway.

Neil shrugged. "Maybe we could do something."

"Well . . . maybe," Andy replied evasively. "I have to go." He turned to head into the crowd.

Suddenly, Andy went sprawling. A snicker of laughter reached Neil's ears, and he looked up to see Charlie Cashman standing there.

"Oh, I'm so sorry, Andy," Charlie said with mock sincerity. "I didn't mean to trip you."

Neil felt his heart start racing. Paralyzed, he watched Andy stare up at Charlie from the floor. In the next instant, Andy leaped up and tackled Charlie. They both went flying over.

A yell of surprise and excitement went up from the crowd. Everyone parted to make room for the two boys, who were grappling on the floor. Neil realized he should stop the fight, but he couldn't move.

"What's going on here!" Roger Collins, the English teacher, fought his way through the crowd. "Hey, break it up, guys! Move it!"

Mr. Collins grabbed Charlie by the arms and pulled him to his feet. Andy stood up and backed away. Both boys looked disheveled, but neither one was hurt.

Charlie started laughing. "It was nothing, Mr. Collins," he said, wiping his nose.

Andy was breathing heavily, and the look he gave Charlie was murderous.

"What's wrong with you, Charlie?" Mr. Collins demanded angrily. "Did you start this?"

Charlie just sniffed, trying to catch his breath, and Andy didn't say anything. The crowd was silent and expectant.

With a disgusted look on his face, Mr. Collins took Charlie's arm. "Get over to Mr. Cooper's office," he said, giving him a small shove down the hall. "I'll be there in a few minutes."

"Sure, boss," Charlie said. He straightened his shoulders and strolled confidently in the direction of the principal's office. As he passed Andy, he smiled and said, "Later."

"Get out of here, Cashman!" Mr. Collins warned.

Charlie raised his hand. "I'm going. I'm going." Then he deliberately stepped on Andy's books, which were scattered across the hall floor.

Without a word, Andy picked up his books. Then he shoved his way through the crowd in the opposite direction. In another moment, the hall was filled with the sounds of chattering, bustling students again.

"Neil?" Mr. Collins put one hand on Neil's shoulder.

"What?" Neil shook his head, as though coming out of a daze. "What?"

Mr. Collins was looking at him. "What's going on here? Do you know?"

Mr. Collins was one of the younger, more popular teachers at Sweet Valley High, and Neil liked him. But it wasn't easy to talk about what was going on, especially since he had such conflicting feelings. "It's Charlie and—it's kind of hard to explain," he began.

The English teacher glanced around and then nodded his head toward an open door. "Come in here," he said. He led Neil into the empty classroom. "Now, I'm sure it *is* hard to explain, but just give it your best shot."

Neil stared at the floor. His mind was a blank.

"Come on," Mr. Collins prompted. "Is something going on between Charlie and Andy that I should know about?"

Neil shrugged, "Charlie has it in for Andy, that's all," he said. "He just doesn't like him."

"Doesn't like him? Why?" Mr. Collins looked at Neil intently, his arms folded. "Because he's black?"

Neil glanced up swiftly. "Well, yeah, kind of . . ."

"Look, I know you and Andy are friends," Mr. Collins went on.

Neil didn't comment.

"And I also know Andy probably won't say anything. So keep an eye out for him. If Charlie gets out of line again, let me know." The teacher arched his eyebrows expectantly. "OK?"

"Sure," Neil mumbled. He shifted his books uneasily. "Look, I have to get to class."

Mr. Collins sighed. "OK. Go ahead. Keep me in the picture, though. I want to know what's going on."

"I will," Neil said and headed for the door.

He knew that Mr. Collins was one of the best, most trustworthy teachers at Sweet Valley High. And as the newspaper adviser, Mr. Collins had Penny's respect and friendship. Penny would definitely agree with the teacher's advice.

But Neil wasn't sure. Andy wanted to do it *his* way, alone. And it looked like that meant walling Neil out of his life. Well, Neil was beginning to think he would rather go it alone, too. He was willing to give Andy the benefit of the doubt, and try one more time to mend their friendship. But after that, it was every man for himself.

"I heard about the fight," Penny said when Neil joined her at lunch. "Charlie really makes me furious. Didn't he trip Andy?"

Neil didn't answer for a moment. He opened a carton of milk and took a swallow. "Yeah," he said when he was finished.

Penny groaned. "How can people be that way?"

"I don't know," Neil said with a sigh. He looked at her. "Listen, I was thinking of asking Andy and Tracy to go with us to the movies tonight. Would you mind?"

"Of course not! That's a great idea."

Neil stood up abruptly. "I'm going to ask him now. He's usually in the band room this period, practicing."

"OK," Penny said. "Are you coming back to finish lunch?"

Neil looked at his roast beef sandwich. He had no appetite at all. "No. I'll see you later."

Before she could say anything more, he picked up his tray, put it on the conveyer belt, then hurried out of the cafeteria. If Andy wanted to be friends, fine. Otherwise, there was no point in trying any longer. Neil walked quickly down the corridor behind the auditorium. The sound of a French horn came through one of the closed doors.

Neil pushed the door open, and Andy looked up, a startled expression on his face. He lowered his horn slowly to his lap.

"What's up?" Andy asked in a guarded tone.

Neil took a chair and turned it around so he could straddle it. He rubbed his palms on the knees of his jeans, then rested them on the chair back. "Penny and I are going to the movies tonight. Why don't you and Tracy come?" The words came out in a rush.

Andy picked up his horn and ran through a quick scale. "No, thanks," he said after a moment.

Neil took a couple of slow breaths. "Why not?" he asked.

"Listen," Andy said, giving Neil a long, steady stare. "I don't need it, OK? You don't have to be nice to me out of guilt. Thanks anyway, but I don't need you to babysit me." He held Neil's gaze for another few seconds and then picked up his horn and continued practicing his scales.

Neil could feel himself growing angry. "Oh, come on, Andy! I can't believe you would think—"

"I'm kind of busy," Andy cut in. "You can close the door on your way out."

"I'm not just going to leave. I mean, I feel like you're blaming me, too, for what Charlie's been doing. I thought we were—"

"I said," Andy repeated in a stony voice, "you can close the door on your way out."

Without a word, Neil stood up, pushed the chair sharply away, and strode out of the room. He slammed the door behind him.

By the time Neil picked Penny up at her house, he was in a terrible mood.

"Andy and Tracy aren't coming?" Penny asked as she climbed into the front seat with him.

"Right. Andy didn't want to," Neil told her.

"That's too bad," Penny went on. "We haven't been out with them in a while." She gave Neil a concerned look. "I hope all this

75

stuff with Charlie isn't getting in the way of your relationship."

"Well, it is," Neil fumed. "If you ask me, Andy's being a complete jerk about the whole thing. Look, I don't want to talk about it, OK?"

Neil was glad they were going to a movie where he could just stare at the screen and forget about everything that had been going on. But once they got to the theater, he couldn't concentrate on the movie. The longer he sat in the darkened theater, the angrier he became.

Andy's been treating me like dirt, he thought indignantly. *He thinks he's better than anyone. He acts like since he's black, everyone else is wrong, never him.*

It seemed to Neil that Andy was acting more self-righteous and judgmental than anyone else, even Charlie. At least Charlie was only picking on one person. Andy was taking it out on everyone, especially Neil.

Well you can forget it, Jenkins. Just forget it. I don't need this kind of crap from anyone.

"What's wrong?" Penny whispered.

Startled, Neil glanced at her. "What?"

"You're breathing in a really weird way," she told him. "Are you all right?"

"Yes," Neil said. He tried to bring his breath-

76

ing under control. He found he was clenching his fists, and he released them slowly.

"Are you thinking about Andy?" Penny asked quietly.

Neil didn't say anything.

"I know you must be upset," she went on.

"I'm fine," Neil lied.

After that, Neil tried to pay attention to the movie but it was useless. He was upset about Andy, all right. But what he really was was mad. He was furious with Andy for rejecting his friendship.

He shifted irritably in his seat.

"Do you want to leave?" Penny asked.

"Actually, if you don't care, I *would* like to get out of here," Neil said.

They ducked over and scrambled out to the aisle. When they reached the mall lobby, Neil looked at Penny and smiled. But he wasn't very convincing.

"You're really worried, aren't you?" Penny asked in a concerned voice.

"Well . . . Penny, would you mind if we just skipped getting something to eat?" Neil asked. "I think I'd rather go home."

Penny gave him a tender smile. "Sure. I understand."

Together, they headed for the parking lot at

the back of the mall. Neil always used it because it was less crowded than the main lot, and he could usually get a good spot near the entrance. As they stepped through the double doors, a sudden movement under a lamppost at the far end of the lot caught his eye.

"What's going on over there?" Penny asked sharply.

Several boys were rocking a car and shouting angrily. Neil and Penny couldn't hear exactly what they were saying, nor could they make out any faces, but it looked like a violent scene.

"Is there someone in that car?" Penny asked. Suddenly she clutched Neil's arm. "Oh, no! I think there is!"

"Go back inside," Neil said to Penny, pushing her backward. "Call the cops. It looks like those guys are going to pound someone pretty bad."

"But—" Penny bit her lip and then nodded. She hurried away.

Neil started running toward the shouting group. The first person he recognized was Charlie Cashman.

And then he saw Andy's father's car.

Eight

Neil stopped in his tracks, staring in horror at the scene unfolding in front of him. While he watched, the gang of boys dragged Andy from the car and closed in on him like a pack of wolves going in for the kill.

What happened next seemed as if it were in slow motion. For a moment, Neil stood frozen. When he finally started to move, he felt as if he, too, were stumbling forward in slow motion. By the time he was near enough for Charlie to notice him, Andy was on the ground, curled up and unconscious.

"Freemount," Charlie said in a challenging tone.

Neil stared at him, his mind a blank. A slow smile spread across Charlie's face. He was flushed and grinning.

"This is your chance," Charlie said. "Take your best shot."

"What?" Neil's voice cracked. He couldn't look at the body slumped on the ground in front of him.

"Come on," Charlie invited. "I know you've been wanting to do it. He's been treating you like you're some kind of fool."

"Yeah," Jerry McAllister chimed in. "The creep. We had to teach him a lesson."

One of the other boys lifted Andy by the shoulders. Andy's head lolled to one side, and he let out a groan.

"This is your chance to pay him back for all the lousy things he's been saying to you," Charlie went on. His voice was earnest, coaxing. "He's been taking advantage of you, Neil. He only cares about himself. That's all he ever cared about. That's why he treats you like a chump."

All the feelings of hurt, anger, and confusion that had been swirling around in Neil's head suddenly crystallized into a pounding need to get back at Andy.

"Go on," Charlie said, his eyes glittering. "Hit him. Hit him!"

Neil took a deep breath and stared at Andy. He raised his arm to hit his former friend. But just as his fist went shooting toward Andy, something inside Neil snapped, and he realized with horror what he was doing. He tried to stop himself, to pull back, but it was too late. His fist connected with Andy's solar plexus, and Andy let out a breathless grunt.

"Way to go, Freemount," Jerry said with a chuckle. "Two points."

While the others hooted with laughter, Neil stared in horror at Andy's unconscious form. Suddenly, he felt so weak with shame and remorse that he thought he would collapse. He reached blindly for the side of the car to hold himself up.

"Try for the extra point," Charlie goaded.

"What have I done?" Neil choked and turned away. He stumbled, then started running for his car.

"Neil!" Charlie yelled. "Stick around! We just started!"

Laughter followed Neil. He felt so over-whelmed by what he had done that all he could think about was getting away. Gasping, he wrenched open his car door and started the engine. He pulled out of the parking lot with such speed that his tires squealed.

He wanted to drive away and never come back, never see Penny again, never see his friends or his family, never know how badly Andy was hurt. He felt numb with shock at what he had done.

Blindly, Neil drove out to the highway and kept going. His car was swerving wildly. Neil could hardly remember how to drive. He knew he shouldn't have left Penny, but he didn't know what else to do. Hot tears spilled down his cheeks, and a breathless, suffocating sensation made him gasp for air. Sobbing, he pulled the car to the side of the road, opened the door, and threw up.

He felt as though he had just stepped over the brink into a bottomless pit. There was no turning back now, no way to undo what he had done.

Neil spent the rest of the weekend in his room. He told his mother he was sick and couldn't come to the phone. He knew Penny called several times. The messages his mother relayed simply said, "Please call." Neil couldn't bear to face her. He knew she would be angry and demand an explanation.

Neither of his parents asked any questions, and Neil was grateful for that. But he knew he was only postponing the inevitable.

It surprised him that the police didn't call, or Andy, or Charlie—no one who had anything to do with the incident on Friday night except for Penny. It was as though nothing had happened. Neil went to school on Monday morning curious, but full of sick anxiety.

"Neil!" Penny ran up to him when he reached his locker.

He looked at her, a stricken expression on his face. He couldn't speak.

"Where did you go on Friday night?" she asked. "I waited for over an hour after the police got there. Why didn't you come back?"

"I—" Neil's throat closed up on him. He started shaking his head.

"I guess when you realized it was Andy, you went to get help, too," Penny went on in a worried tone. "It's a good thing the police got there so quickly. They told me the guys who did it scattered when they arrived." She looked up at him. "Do you have any idea who was beating him up? He won't talk to the police. He won't say a word."

Neil stared at her. He couldn't quite take in what she was saying. Did Andy know about him? Did anyone know?

"Oh, Neil," Penny said. "Isn't it terrible?"

Neil nodded, still feeling dazed.

"Everyone is completely shocked," Penny continued. "I just can't believe something like that could happen here. I thought it only happened in big cities, like New York or L.A., but I guess I was naive."

Neil nodded again. His heart was pounding deafeningly in his ears. He really couldn't think straight at all. There was no angry mob of people waiting to accuse him and cast him out. And Penny was so caught up in talking about the whole thing that she didn't even seem mad at him for deserting her.

"I'm writing an editorial for *The Oracle*," Penny went on. They started walking together down the hall. "If only—"

"Listen," Neil broke in. He had to tell her, but he didn't know how to begin. "Listen, I-I'm sorry I didn't come back to get you. It's just that . . . I don't know what came over me—"

"I was kind of mad at first," she admitted. "But then I realized . . . Well, it must have been really hard on you, seeing him get beaten up like that."

The look on Penny's face was so understanding that Neil groaned. He couldn't bring himself to tell her. She would hate him, and he couldn't face that now. Not yet.

"I'm going to be late for class," he said, moving away.

Elizabeth Wakefield walked up to join Penny. Following her friend's gaze, she commented. "Neil looks really shaken up."

"I know," Penny agreed. "Andy is one of his best friends. I guess it was a shock when he realized he was getting beaten up."

"This whole thing is so awful," Elizabeth said. "Does Neil know who did it?"

"I don't—think so," Penny faltered. She squeezed her eyes shut and let out a frustrated sigh. "I'm just so furious. It makes me want to scream."

"I know what you mean. How could something like that happen here?" Elizabeth said. "I just wish Andy would talk about it," she went on. "I heard he wouldn't stay overnight in the hospital, even though he was hurt pretty badly. Is it true he won't talk to the police?"

Penny nodded.

"This is turning into a nightmare!" Elizabeth exclaimed.

"Liz!" Jessica's voice reached her from down the hallway. "Wait up!"

Elizabeth and Penny waited for Jessica to catch up.

"Can you believe this?" Jessica's eyes were wide with shock. "Everybody's talking about it. It's like something from the newspapers or something. Liz, I can't believe I didn't take you more seriously when you told me that stuff about Andy's locker and everything. Do you think Charlie Cashman did this, too?

"I'm going to start a petition," Jessica rushed on, without waiting for an answer. She waved a sheet of notebook paper in front of them. "Just to say we think this is a terrible thing and we're on Andy's side."

"I'll sign it," Penny said. "I'll be first."

Elizabeth watched them writing. "We should also have some kind of racism awareness program," she mused. "I think it's really important. Most racism isn't even as obvious as beating someone up."

"It's terrible when it takes something like this to make people aware," Penny said. She pushed her hair back in an impatient gesture. "It's time for class. Let's talk about what we should do at lunchtime."

Elizabeth and Jessica nodded, and the three girls headed for their classes.

In both chemistry and French, the two classes that Elizabeth and Jessica shared, people were talking about the incident. And as the morning passed, more and more people were discussing it. When Jessica walked into sociology, everyone in the class was speaking in hushed whispers. Every face wore a shocked, outraged expression.

"Listen up, people," their teacher, Ms. Jacobi, said. "Instead of talking about urban planning today, I want to do an exercise with you about prejudice."

Jessica raised her eyebrows and glanced next to her. Cara Walker, who took sociology with Jessica and was also the long-time girlfriend of Jessica's older brother Steven, shrugged and returned her questioning look. Word had spread quickly. It appeared that Sweet Valley High was taking the attack against Andy very seriously.

"Now, would everyone with blue or gray eyes please raise his or her hand?" the teacher went on.

Curious, Jessica raised her hand in the air. On her other side, Amy Sutton, raised her hand, too. Several other students in the room did as well. They were outnumbered by at least two to one.

"Fine." Ms. Jacobi folded her arms and looked very stern. "Now, because of this totally arbitrary characteristic—your eye color—you people are now second-class citizens."

There was a collective gasp from all the people with blue eyes. "What do you mean?" Jessica asked.

"Who said you could talk?" the teacher said sharply.

Jessica felt her face turning red. She saw that Amy looked stunned. Everyone else in the room looked puzzled and embarrassed.

"The rest of you," Ms. Jacobi went on in a friendly tone, "may speak in any way you like to the Light-Eyes. Treat them as badly as you want to. They don't deserve better."

Her heart pounding, Jessica looked around the room. The kids with dark eyes looked uncomfortable, but not nearly as uneasy as her fellow Light-Eyes. For several minutes, nobody spoke.

"I want to sit there," Cara said to Amy.

Amy picked up her books and moved from her desk. "Where should I sit?" she asked.

"I don't care," Cara said. "Just not near me."

"Good, Cara," the teacher said. "That's the spirit."

As Amy stepped aside, she caught Cara's eye.

"Sorry," Cara whispered. She shrugged.

"I understand," Amy whispered back. She looked at Jessica, who was arguing with Maria Santelli.

"No, I will not pick up your books!" Jessica said indignantly.

Maria raised her hand. "Jessica won't do what I say."

The teacher scowled at Jessica. "Did you knock Miss Santelli's books on the floor?" she demanded.

"No!" Jessica said.

"You're a liar," the teacher sneered. "All you Light-Eyes are liars."

Somebody at the back of the room laughed. Ken Matthews, who also had blue eyes, was blushing.

"Go sharpen this pencil for me," Kirk Anderson said to Ken in an arrogant tone.

Ken stood up and glared at Kirk, then went to the pencil sharpener. He turned the handle with swift, violent cranks.

Jessica sat down on a chair in the corner, hugging her books to her chest. She couldn't believe how horrible it felt to be singled out so suddenly and abused simply because of the color of her eyes. Even though she knew it was an experiment, she still felt awful.

It was truly frightening to see the way her classmates with dark eyes were behaving. Some people looked apologetic, but almost everyone was getting into it to some degree. The power to dominate seemed to go to their heads almost instantly.

For the rest of the class, Jessica, Amy, and the other Light-Eyes were victims of the worst kind of scorn, criticism, and ridicule. The teacher announced at one point that all the Light-Eyes would have to sit at the back of the room and would not be allowed to speak under any circumstances. Jessica sat next to Amy.

This is what is feels like, she told herself. *This is how it feels to be discriminated against.*

She was furious and she sat with her arms folded across her chest, a stubborn pout on her face.

"This stinks," she whispered to Amy. "How come we have to do this? It doesn't make any sense to pick on us."

"No talking," someone at the front of the room ordered.

Amy gave her a silent look. It made just as

much sense to pick on people with light eyes as it did to pick on people with brown skin— or a different religion, or an unusual accent, or anything else.

Finally, five minutes before the class was over, Ms. Jacobi made another announcement.

"OK. That's all the discrimination I can stand dealing out for one day," she said. "Now, let's talk about what we just did here."

Jessica stood up immediately and strode to her usual seat. "I think this was the stupidest experiment," she complained.

"Why?" the teacher asked.

"Because it wasn't *fair*," Jessica said. "Why wasn't everybody discriminated against?"

"Then it wouldn't be discrimination," Ken said.

"Dark eyes are always a majority," Ms. Jacobi explained. "So now you know what it feels like to be in a minority, and how it feels to suffer because of it."

"I didn't know it would hurt so much," one of the Light-Eyes called out. "I felt like crying."

The teacher nodded. "How about some of the Dark-Eyes?" she asked. "How did you feel?"

"Weird," Winston Egbert offered. "I mean, I thought I wouldn't want to be mean to them, but it was pretty easy. That makes me kind of nervous," he added, looking around the room. Some of the others nodded.

"I guess this gives you something to think about, doesn't it?" Ms. Jacobi asked in a quiet voice.

Jessica looked at the petition sitting on top of her books. In the past thirty minutes, it had become even more important to her. Now she knew a little bit of what it felt like to be on the receiving end of bigotry and prejudice.

And it made her furious.

Nine

Neil avoided the cafeteria at lunchtime that day. He knew everyone would be talking about the attack on Andy, and he was sure his guilt would be written all over his face. Each time someone spoke to him, he jumped nervously, expecting to be accused of taking part in the beating. But so far, no one had said anything. Apparently, Charlie and the other guys who had been at the parking lot hadn't told anyone.

But Neil felt sick with nervousness. He roamed the halls aimlessly during his lunch period, and the rest of the day he only felt worse. It was torture. People were treating him like some kind of hero. Everyone, including his own girlfriend, assumed he had tried to *help* Andy. Neil was the only one who knew what a terrible fraud he was.

When the last bell rang, Neil made a quick stop at his locker, then hurried home without stopping to talk to anyone. He went straight to his room, put a cassette in his tape deck, and sat brooding at his desk. He was still sitting there when he heard his father's car pull into the driveway shortly after five o'clock and the front door open and close.

"Hey, Neil," Mr. Freemount called up to him. "I've got a surprise for you!"

Neil slowly went downstairs.

"I know you've been kind of under the weather lately," his father said. "I've got just the ticket to turn things around."

Mr. Freemount was holding out a pair of tickets. Neil took one and read it. It was for the USC football game that evening.

"What?" He didn't understand.

"We have to hurry if we're going to make it on time," his father went on. "I have to tell you, I am really looking forward to this. We haven't seen a game together in what—a couple of years?"

Neil nodded his head mechanically. He was thrown completely off balance by his father's sudden camaraderie. "Sounds great, Dad," he managed to say.

On the long drive to the stadium, Neil was quiet, staring out the window, trying to organize his thoughts.

Of all evenings that his father could have picked to treat him to a football game, why that night? Neil didn't know. But suddenly he didn't care.

All at once he felt a burden lifted off his shoulders. For a couple of hours, anyway, he didn't have to think about what he'd done to Andy or what he could do about it. He breathed a sigh of relief and sank down into the seat.

"Excited?" his father asked.

Neil smiled. "Yeah, Dad."

"Good." Mr. Freemount reached over and ruffled Neil's hair.

Once they reached the stadium, Neil forgot all about the turmoil of the last several days. He and his father whooped like a couple of kids as they headed for their seats. Once the game started, they analyzed every play. Neil felt good to just be acting like any other high school student, without the weight of the world resting on him.

"Listen, son," Mr. Freemount said during halftime. He took a bit of his hot dog and chewed for a moment. "I want to talk about something serious."

"Sure," Neil said. He started to feel nervous. Was there some terrible retribution in store for him?

Mr. Freemount glanced over his shoulder and then dropped his voice. "I heard from Frank Cashman this morning after you left for school."

Neil felt his stomach plunge. He swallowed hard and stared straight ahead, pretending to watch the halftime show.

I should have known it would happen, he told himself bleakly.

"I think I know how you felt," his father went on in a low, sympathetic tone. "I don't blame you one bit."

Neil turned startled eyes to his father. "What? I—"

"Now, hear me out," Mr. Freemount cut in. "First of all, I want to say that hitting a man while he's down—well, that's not exactly fair and square."

There was a dull pounding in Neil's ears. He couldn't answer.

"But I know your heart was in the right place," his father concluded.

Neil just sat there and stared at his father.

For a moment, he wasn't sure he had heard correctly. He blinked and shook his head. "What?" he finally said.

"I know, I know," Mr. Freemount said, putting his hand on Neil's shoulder. "You probably felt a little worried about it, but I know Andy had it coming."

"Dad—" Neil's voice came out strained. "They—we—*beat him up*."

Mr. Freemount shrugged. "So you were a little rough on him. But you can be sure of one thing. He's learned his lesson now. Whoa—second half's starting."

The crowd let out a roar of excitement as the teams ran back onto the field. Neil felt dizzy. He tried to draw a breath, but he felt as though he were choking. Beside him, his father was standing up and clapping, shouting to the players.

I can't believe this, Neil thought. It was like a nightmare. His father was *praising* him for beating up Andy. It was sickening.

Neil sat in stunned silence throughout the rest of the game. All he could think about was Andy. He knew he couldn't live with himself even if no one ever found out he had punched Andy. Setting his teeth, Neil decided to go to Andy's as soon as he got home, no matter how late it was. It was time to come clean about it.

"Some game, eh?" Mr. Freemount chuckled as the final buzzer sounded. "We should do this more often."

Neil looked blankly at his father. "No, thanks," he said.

"What?" Mr. Freemount smiled knowingly. "Neil, don't take this incident to heart too much. These things happen."

There was nothing Neil could say. When he looked at his father, he felt as if he were a long distance away. He knew he would never be able to talk to him again. Neil maintained a dull, dazed silence all the way back to Sweet Valley. He felt completely drained.

"Let me out here," he said when they stopped at a light in the middle of town. He started opening his door.

"Neil—" Mr. Freemount took his elbow for a moment. "Where are you going? It's eleven o'clock."

"I know," Neil said. He pulled his arm free and stepped out of the car. "I'll be home soon."

His father frowned at him. "Look, Neil," he said in a blustery tone, "don't you go acting all high and mighty with me. I know what you did. You're no better than anyone else." He put the car back into gear, and Neil watched him drive away.

Neil didn't know what to think. But he was sure of one thing. He had to tell Andy the truth. Squaring his shoulders, he turned in the direction of Andy's neighborhood. He almost faltered and turned to head back home, but he made himself keep going.

Soon, he was standing on the sidewalk in front of the Jenkinses', staring up at the familiar house. The living room lights were on, so Neil knew that someone was still up.

Do it, he told himself firmly. But he could hardly make his feet move. After a couple of minutes he walked up the steps and knocked on the door.

"Neil!" Mrs. Jenkins opened the door, and light spilled out into Neil's face.

"I'm sorry to drop by so late, Mrs. Jenkins," Neil began.

"Don't give it another thought. I'm a night owl. Am I glad to see you! Come on in. Andy! Guess who's here!"

"Well, well," Mr. Jenkins said, coming into the hall. He shook his head. "Your friend Penny called, told us how you two called the police. We really appreciate it, Neil. It means a lot to us."

Neil stared at them. His mouth had gone completely dry. To save his life, he could not make himself speak.

"Go on into Andy's room," Mrs. Jenkins went on warmly. "He'll be so glad to see you."

Nodding mutely, Neil walked down the hallway and knocked on Andy's door. Then he opened it slowly.

Andy was reading in bed. There was a bandage on his head, and Neil could see a few scratches and bruises.

Andy looked up with a wide smile when Neil walked in. "Hey!" he said.

Just get it over with, said the voice in Neil's head. He tried not to wince, but it was really upsetting to see just how badly Andy was hurt.

"Andy—I—" Neil choked.

"Listen," Andy broke in. He looked somber. "I'm really glad you came. I wanted to talk to you, but I felt like such a jerk I couldn't get up the nerve to call you."

Neil blinked. "What?"

Andy shifted on the bed, sitting up straighter. "Listen, about the way I've been acting lately. I've been lying here thinking, and I realized that that jerk Charlie got me so confused, I was being as much of a racist as he was. I know we're friends, and I was a major fool not to appreciate you. It doesn't matter what color either of us is."

"But—" Neil whispered.

"But you stuck by me, anyway," Andy went on. "I know you guys were the ones who called the cops."

"But you don't understand," Neil said. He had to grit his teeth to keep his purpose clearly in mind. "You don't—"

"Don't worry about it," Andy said, smiling again. "You did the right thing. That's what I care about."

Neil just stared at Andy. This was so twisted he couldn't believe it. Before he could say anything, the door opened again and Mrs. Jenkins came in.

"I brought you some sodas," she said, putting two cans down by Andy's bed. "And some pound cake."

"Thanks, Mom," Andy said.

While Mrs. Jenkins fussed over them, adjusting Andy's pillows and praising Neil, Neil took a slice of cake, broke off a piece, and put it in his mouth. He chewed it slowly, but he couldn't taste a thing.

"Let's start all over," Andy said as he picked up his soda. "We're friends, all that black versus white garbage doesn't make any difference.

We'll show everyone we're above all of that." He tapped his soda can against Neil's and then drank.

Neil stood up suddenly. "I have to go," he said. He couldn't meet Andy's eyes. "It's late. My folks will be worried. I just wanted to see if you were OK."

"Thanks. I'll see you in school." Andy held his hand out.

Tell him! yelled the voice inside Neil's head.

Slowly, he reached his hand out and took Andy's. They shook silently. Then Neil turned and hurried out of the room. He was down the hall and out the front door before Andy's parents even realized he was gone. Once he hit the street, he started running.

I couldn't do it. I couldn't do it. I'm a coward and a fake, Neil told himself furiously.

His breath was coming in harsh gasps from running so fast. He stumbled to a halt next to some garbage cans by the curb. Panting, hating himself, he kicked one of them over, then grabbed another one and threw it as hard as he could. Garbage scattered, and a dog started barking somewhere.

Then Neil turned and started the long walk home.

Ten

Elizabeth brought the rough draft of her survey article to lunch on Tuesday and sat down at a table with a group of her friends.

"Hi, Enid," she said.

Enid took a sip of her apple juice. "What's up?"

"Tell me what you think of this sentence," Elizabeth began. " 'Survey results show a surprising number of students at this school, especially girls, feel they are discriminated against.' "

"What about it?" Enid asked, arching her eyebrows. "It's true, isn't it?"

"What do you mean, girls are discriminated

against?" Aaron Dallas spoke up. He made a face. "Girls get all the breaks. Always."

Dana Larson, who was sitting next to him, let out a gasp. "You're kidding me, right? Girls do *not* get all the breaks."

"I think a lot of girls on the sports teams feel that way," Elizabeth explained to Aaron. "They say they get less money for equipment, less coverage in the news, less support from other students."

Aaron and Ken Matthews exchanged knowing looks. "Yeah," Ken said. "But since when are girls' sports really as important as the guys' teams? There's no Homecoming field hockey game, I noticed."

"Right." Aaron let out a laugh, and Dana punched him in the shoulder.

"Do you think girls aren't as good athletes as boys?" Penny asked. She had just joined the group, and overheard Ken's remark.

"Well . . ." Ken and Aaron both had wide grins on their faces, but they knew they would be in trouble if they answered Penny's question truthfully.

Elizabeth put her elbows on the table and leaned forward. She was surprised and a little bit indignant that the boys were treating the discussion as a big joke. "What would you say if a girl tried out for varsity quarterback?" she asked.

There was a startled silence. Finally, Ken shook his head. "I'd say you have a good sense of humor, Liz." Aaron laughed again.

"I'm totally serious," she insisted. She thought back to that anonymous answer to her survey, the girl who wanted to play football. Elizabeth hoped whoever it was would try out and that she would make the team.

Ken gave the other boys a smug grin. Until a few months ago, he had been Sweet Valley High's quarterback, one of the best the school had ever had. Then he had been in a terrible car accident. A drunk driver had forced him off the road, and Ken had crashed his car. As a result, he received a serious head injury that had made him temporarily blind. Scott Trost, a sophomore at Sweet Valley High, had replaced Ken as quarterback. It had been a bad few months for Ken, but now his eyesight was almost completely restored, and he was getting stronger all the time. Everyone, including Ken, assumed he was a shoo-in for the first-string position next season. Obviously, the thought of a girl competing against him for the spot struck him as preposterous.

"Sorry, Liz," Ken said. "There are lots of

sports that girls can be good at, but football just isn't one of them."

"Nice condescending tone there," Penny muttered under her breath. Elizabeth nodded her agreement.

Olivia Davidson, the *Oracle*'s arts editor, had quietly joined the group and was listening to the debate. "Ken, do girls make good sprinters?" Olivia asked. Ken shrugged. "How about strategy?" she went on. "Can girls be good at strategy?"

"Sure," Ken said, looking impatient.

"Well how about throwing?" Dana put in. "There are plenty of girls who have a pretty good arm, wouldn't you say?"

Ken rolled his eyes. "I guess."

"Then why couldn't a girl be a quarterback?" Enid asked, catching their point. "'What else do you need?"

"It's totally different," Ken protested. "You've got it all wrong."

"Why?" Penny pressed. "In what way?"

Ken and Aaron both looked embarrassed and uncomfortable. "There's just a difference," Aaron said.

"In your head, maybe," Dana retorted. "This is just sex discrimination, pure and simple, guys."

"It is not!" Ken protested. "It is not discrimination at all!"

"Oh, yeah?" Olivia said, her eyes flashing. "I bet you think Andy Jenkins getting beat up wasn't discrimination, either."

Nobody spoke. Elizabeth looked at the faces around the lunch table. Everyone was solemn. Elizabeth didn't know about anyone else, but she felt a little guilty. She knew she had never hurt anyone, but *some* white people had, and she was ashamed to be associated with them.

Suddenly Enid jostled her elbow and looked pointedly over her shoulder. Elizabeth followed her friend's gaze. Andy Jenkins and Tracy Gilbert had just gone through the cafeteria line and were standing, trays in hand, looking for a place to sit. For a moment, there seemed to be a hush in the lunchroom. Then the noise started up again.

"Andy! Tracy!" Penny called. "Over here!"

Andy turned and saw her and lifted his hand. Then he and Tracy headed for their table.

A chorus of greetings met the couple as they sat down. Everyone asked how Andy was, and said they were glad he was back. Andy seemed grateful for their concern.

"I'm OK," he said.

"Andy," Elizabeth began, "I just want you

to know that just because some people are jerks . . ."

Andy nodded and gave her a smile. "I know. Believe me, I know. In fact, in a way, things are a lot clearer now. You know, you just have to take people for who they are, not what they are."

"That's so true," Penny agreed fervently.

He glanced at her. "Where's Neil? I haven't seen him all day."

"I'm—not sure," Penny began. She glanced toward the door and frowned.

Elizabeth noticed the doubtful sound in Penny's voice. It did seem odd that Neil wasn't with her. He usually was. But he was probably just studying in the library or something.

Winston Egbert came up behind Tracy and Andy. "The ceremony to give out the science and math awards is tomorrow during fourth period," he reminded everyone. He grinned at Andy. "You'll be cleaning up, Mr. Scholarship."

Andy tried to look modest. "I just do my best," he began.

Some of the other kids said, "Sure, Jenkins," in teasing voices and rolled their eyes. Andy laughed.

"There are other people getting awards, you know," he pointed out. "It's not just for me."

"Right," Dana said. "Like me. I'm getting the most-likely-to-blow-up-the-lab award."

Everyone laughed. Soon, the conversation at the table turned to other topics. Plans for a beach party were underway, and everyone seemed anxious that Andy come. Elizabeth felt a surge of warmth when she looked at her friends. They all wanted to reassure Andy that they liked him. And it wasn't just because of his race. That would be reverse discrimination, which was just as bad. They all genuinely liked him because he was a likable guy, and he seemed to recognize their friendship for what it was.

Still smiling, Elizabeth turned to Penny again. But Penny looked preoccupied and distant.

"What's wrong?" Elizabeth asked in a low voice.

Penny shook her head absently. "Nothing. It's just—I'm wondering where Neil is. He's been out of it since the weekend. We haven't seen much of each other since then. I know he's been really shaken up by the whole thing, but I just wish he could talk to me about it more. I wish he were here now."

"Don't worry about it, Penny," Elizabeth said

sympathetically. "I'm sure he just needs a little time to get over it."

Penny considered Elizabeth's words. "You're right," she said with determination. "I guess I'm just being selfish. I'm sure he'll be back to his old self in a few days."

Neil wandered out in front of the school during lunch period and sat alone under a tree. He had a wax-coated soda cup in his hand, and he nervously picked at the wax while he stared into the distance. Everything was all wrong.

Andy was back in school, which was great, of course. What wasn't great for Neil was that everyone thought *he* was a hero, including Andy. But Neil knew the truth. He had been trying to avoid Andy all day, but Andy kept tracking him down. It was torture to see the smile of gratitude and friendship on Andy's face.

"Hey, Neil."

Neil turned around. It was Charlie. Neil's spirits sank even further as he watched the other boy stroll up. "What?" Neil said shortly, before Charlie had a chance to speak.

"What kind of an attitude is that?" Charlie

asked, holding his hands out wide. "I just wanted to stop and say hello, buddy."

Neil looked away. "I'm not your buddy, all right?"

"All right," Charlie said in a placid tone. "We're just soldiers in the same army, something like that, right?" He grinned maliciously.

When Neil didn't say anything, Charlie settled down on the grass. "So, it looks like Jenkins didn't learn his lesson yet. He's getting a hero's welcome all over this school."

"What about it?" Neil said.

He couldn't stop himself from provoking Charlie. He just couldn't believe he had teamed up with this creep to beat up his friend. How could it have happened? He couldn't understand it.

And something else worried him, too. What if someone saw him talking to Charlie? Everyone seemed to take it for granted that Charlie was involved in the beating, even though Andy refused to identify his attackers. And if people saw him and Charlie together, they might put two and two together . . .

Neil glanced nervously over his shoulder. He wanted to get up and walk away. But something told him to be careful. Apparently Charlie hadn't told anyone other than his father yet that Neil was more involved than anyone knew. But he might. And Neil knew the situation would get even worse if Andy found out what had really happened from someone else. Neil had to make sure he himself was the one to tell Andy.

"What do you want, Charlie?" Neil asked, trying to keep his voice steady.

Charlie leaned back on his hands and stretched his legs out in front of him. "Nice today, isn't it?"

"What do you want?" Neil shouted.

"Don't get so excited," Charlie said. "It gives you high blood pressure, and you're too young for that." When Neil gave him an angry look, Charlie continued. "OK. See, I figure Andy needs another dose of what he got the other night. Then maybe he and all the other blacks in this town will know we mean business."

Neil felt his chin tremble. He looked away, furious with himself and with Charlie. "Can't you just leave him alone?" he said in a low, intense voice.

"No, Neil. I can't." Charlie shrugged. "I just can't."

"Listen," Neil said, turning to meet Charlie's gaze. "Andy's a great guy. Why don't you just keep away from him?"

Charlie raised his eyebrows. "I noticed that *you* didn't exactly keep away from him the other night."

The color drained from Neil's face. "It was a mistake," he choked out. "It was just a stupid mistake I made."

"Oh." Charlie looked scornful. "A mistake? That's what I'll tell everyone, OK?"

"No!" Neil reached one hand out and then pulled it back. He started shaking his head while a sensation of fear welled up inside him. "Don't—Charlie, don't tell."

Charlie leaned forward, a fierce look on his face. "Listen, Freemount. You're with me or you're not, got it?" he growled. "You can't run with both packs depending on what your mood is that day. Either you help me and the guys teach Andy a lesson, or I just won't have any choice but to turn you in to the police."

Neil felt as if Charlie had just punched him in the stomach. "That would mean turning yourself in," he said.

"Oh, I meant an anonymous tip," Charlie explained. "Besides, I was nowhere near that parking lot on Friday night. I was with my father. Bowling."

Neil was completely flabbergasted. While he stared at him, Charlie stood up and dusted off his jeans. "Catch you later, Neil," he said. "I'm counting on you." He sauntered away.

Neil shook his head. It would be just like Charlie to point the finger at him out of spite.

Neil knew he had to tell the truth soon, before Charlie Cashman did. And that meant he had to go to Andy and set the record straight, no matter what the cost.

Eleven

That evening, Neil picked up the telephone a dozen times to call Andy. But each time, he hung up before he even started to dial the number. He couldn't make himself do it, but the longer he put it off, the worse he felt. By the next morning, he was sick with anxiety.

Neil deliberately waited until the homeroom bell rang before entering the school building so that he wouldn't see Penny or anyone else. It was going to take all of his strength to tell Andy the truth. He was afraid that if he ran into anyone he might back out of telling him again. And he couldn't risk that.

He walked to marine biology class and

stopped at the door. Andy was sitting at his usual desk reading through the textbook. The sight of him nearly made Neil turn around and walk away. He knew that once he admitted what he'd done he would lose Andy's friendship forever, and Penny's, too. And everyone else he cared about would treat him like an outcast.

The only people who would like him would be people like Charlie Cashman.

But it was the price he had to pay. Attacking someone because of his color wasn't something that could be forgiven, or forgotten. Squaring his shoulders, Neil walked into the classroom and set his books down at his desk.

"Hey, Neil," Andy said, looking up. "How's it going?"

Neil's tongue was frozen. He took a deep breath and tried to speak.

"I'm psyched," Andy went on before Neil could say anything. He laughed shyly. "I know it's not cool to brag about getting awards and stuff, but when that ceremony starts today, I'm going to be flying."

"Andy—" Neil cleared his throat. He sat down heavily and stared at Andy. "Why haven't you—why haven't you said who beat you up? Why?"

A frown crossed Andy's face, and he shut his book with a snap. "It's kind of hard to explain," he began. "The thing is, everyone knows anyway, right? Have you noticed the way people are acting toward Cashman?" He made a disgusted face. "He's his own punishment."

"So you're turning the other cheek?" Neil asked, bewildered. It didn't seem right that Charlie would get away with it. And Neil knew that he himself deserved much worse. "I just— I don't get it."

Andy looked serious. "It's not that, exactly. If Cashman tries anything again, I swear I'll nail him. I'll get the NAACP, the American Civil Liberties Union, the cops—I'll get everybody on his case. But I'm pretty sure he won't do anything more."

"I don't think you're right," Neil said desperately, remembering what Charlie had told him the day before. "He's not going to just back off, Andy—"

"Neil, come on," Andy cut in. Then he grinned at Neil. "This is my day. When I get that award, that'll show everyone I can win no matter what kind of stunts they try to pull on me." He punched Neil's shoulder playfully. "Charlie's going to have a fit when I walk up there and shake Cooper's hand. And there's nothing he can do about it. Let's not talk about it anymore, OK? Today, anyway."

The excitement and pride in Andy's face made Neil feel worse than ever. How could he spoil Andy's moment of triumph now? *Telling* Andy would hurt him so much more than that punch in the stomach had. Sick at heart, Neil turned away and opened his biology book. He knew what he had to do, but it seemed just about impossible.

Before fourth period, Penny stopped by Neil's locker.

"Hi, stranger," she said with a smile. "Going to the awards ceremony?"

"Sure," he said. They fell into step together, heading toward the auditorium. Neil was deep in thought and didn't say much. He felt like a hypocrite, going to cheer for Andy when he had helped beat him up. Each step toward the auditorium was harder to make. Finally, at the entrance he stopped.

"What is it?" Penny asked.

He shook his head. "I-I don't feel like going," he admitted.

"What?" Penny looked at him in surprise. "You have to go. You'll miss seeing Andy get his scholarship."

"I know, but—" Neil faltered and stopped. He stared at the floor.

"Are you OK?" Penny asked. "Ever since Andy got beaten up, you've been acting so preoccupied."

Neil could only nod.

"Come on, you guys," Elizabeth said as she hurried past, "or you won't get a seat."

Penny tugged Neil's hand. "Come on. We can talk about it later."

Neil followed her into the auditorium. He felt powerless to do anything at all. He couldn't talk, couldn't think, couldn't act. Oblivious to the excitement all around him, he sat down.

"Is this mike working?" Mr. Cooper asked, tapping the microphone. A wail of feedback screeched out, and dozens of students yelled "Yes" at the same time.

The principal smiled. "Oh, good. Welcome, everyone. I know you don't want to hear my usual speech about how proud the school is of all our award recipients—so to get right to business, here's Mr. Russo to give the first awards."

There was a round of applause as the chemistry teacher walked onto the stage. Neil barely listened as the chemistry awards were handed out. He grew more and more nervous as he waited for the moment when Andy would get his award. He was very glad for Andy. After all, no one deserved the scholarship more. But once Andy had his moment of glory, Neil didn't have any excuse for stalling anymore. He would have to talk to Andy, and he was dreading it.

After Mr. Russo left the podium, other science teachers took turns handing out more awards. Then Mr. Cooper walked on stage again. "Now, before I announce the next award, I want to take this opportunity to say a few words about what happened last weekend."

There was a low murmur throughout the auditorium. Several people turned around to see where Andy Jenkins was. Neil slumped down in his seat. His face felt hot and flushed.

The principal looked serious. "I know I speak for all of us when I say that there is no room for intolerance and prejudice at Sweet Valley High. Every single student here is judged by his or her abilities and merits. And although some of us are better students, or better athletes, or better musicians than others," Mr. Cooper said somberly, "not one person in this school is a better *person* than any other."

A burst of applause broke out, and Mr. Cooper waited for it to die down. "So although it saddens and angers me terribly that one of our students was singled out for abuse, it also gives me great pleasure to know that Andy Jenkins is a young man whose record and potential can mean only one thing: He will go very far in this world even in the face of the prejudices that I'm afraid still linger. And I want to wish him the very best."

Penny stood up and started to clap, and within seconds, everyone in the auditorium was standing to applaud for Andy. Neil dragged himself to his feet and clapped, too, but inside he felt dead.

Mr. Cooper was beckoning to Andy, and Andy climbed the steps up to the stage. The applause doubled in volume while Mr. Cooper shook his hand.

"People! Quiet please!" the principal said sternly into the microphone. After a few more moments the auditorium settled down, and Mr. Cooper handed the microphone to Mr. Archer.

The marine biology teacher was beaming with pride. "Andy Jenkins, it is my great pleasure and honor to award you the Monterey Bay Aquarium Scholarship for Outstanding Achievement in Life Sciences—"

Another raucous burst of applause cut the teacher off, and many people cheered. Everyone rose again for another standing ovation. Andy looked overwhelmed as he took the award certificate from his teacher. Then, a huge smile on his face, he turned to the audience and waved.

"Way to go Andy!" Penny yelled.

Neil forced himself to clap, but he felt completely cut off from all the other students. For the rest of the ceremony, he sat in silence. When the assembly was over, everyone started pouring out of the auditorium and heading for the cafeteria.

"That was really great, wasn't it?" Penny said, walking at Neil's side. "I was so happy for Andy."

Neil didn't answer. He was trying to form the right words in his mind. Until he said them, he was pretty sure he wouldn't be able to say anything else. When he and Penny reached the doorway to the cafeteria, Neil stopped.

"Come on," Penny urged him. Reluctantly, he followed her through the cafeteria line and then over to a big table where Elizabeth, Ken, Todd, and a few of their other friends were sitting. Andy and Tracy were with them.

"Congratulations," Ken was saying to Andy. "Next time I need help in biology, I'm asking you."

"Sure thing," Andy said, opening a can of soda. He looked like he was on top of the world. When he saw Neil, he called out, "Hey, there you are."

Everyone at the table made room for Penny and Neil, shifting chairs and moving closer together. Neil put his tray down next to Andy and then slowly sat down. He forced himself to eat his lunch and listen to the noisy hum of conversation around him. One by one, his friends finished eating and started to leave. Tracy had to go to the library, and she gave Andy a hug and told him she'd see him later. Finally, when only Penny and Andy were left, Neil knew it was time.

He leaned over and whispered to Andy. "We have to talk," he began. "About Friday night—" He stopped.

"What?" Andy asked. His expression became less cheerful at the change of subject.

Neil swallowed hard. "I was—I was there."

"I know you were there," Andy said. "You bailed me out. I'll never forget it."

Penny was watching Neil, and there was a puzzled look in her eyes. He tried to ignore her as he went on.

"No, I was *there*," he repeated painfully.

"I know," Andy said again. But he was beginning to look confused.

Neil squeezed his eyes shut. It was so hard! "No," he said, gritting his teeth. "I was there with the other guys. I hit you, too."

There was a blank look in Andy's eyes that made Neil wild with frustration. "Don't you get it?" he asked. "I hit you, too! I was so mad at you for thinking I was like Charlie that I *was* like him. I hit you."

Andy stared at him for one long moment. The anger and betrayal in his face made Neil want to die. Then Andy stood up and walked away without a word.

Twelve

Pushing her chair back, Penny stood up abruptly. "How could you?" she said with a gasp. Then she turned and ran out of the cafeteria.

Neil groaned. He lunged out of his chair and ran after her. "Penny, wait!"

He had to chase her all the way down the hall and through the school. He caught up with her just as she was about to open the outside door.

"Penny, please," he said, stopping beside her and taking her arm. "Let me explain—"

"Explain what?" she demanded and pulled her arm away. She looked at him with horror.

"Explain how you could turn on your friend and *beat him up*?"

He shook his head. "It doesn't make any sense, I know, and I know you won't forgive me—" he started.

"It's not for me to forgive," she said icily.

"Just listen," he begged. He was desperate for her to understand. "You don't know what I've been going through these past couple of weeks. It was coming at me from all sides—I was so turned around I didn't know who my friends were anymore."

Penny was shaking her head while he spoke. "I don't buy that."

"But that's how it was," he said. He pushed his hair back and tried to collect his thoughts. "I knew the minute I hit him what a stupid, terrible mistake it was. But it was too late. And then everyone assumed I was some kind of life-saver—"

"Yeah, I know *I* did," Penny cut in. She looked away, and Neil saw that there were tears in her eyes.

Neil sniffed hard. "I couldn't let Andy go on thinking that way about me. I had to tell him— it was killing me."

Penny turned to stare at him. "All you did

was try to take care of your own guilty conscience. Telling Andy doesn't make it better."

"I know it doesn't," Neil agreed dejectedly. "It can't make anything right or better—but at least he knows the truth."

"That you're just as bad as Charlie Cashman?" Penny said. She was trembling. "Only not as obvious."

Neil looked away. "Haven't you ever done something you wish you hadn't?" he asked in a low voice. "Something that made you hate yourself?"

"Yes, but not like that," Penny whispered. A tear rolled down her cheek. "Neil, you aren't the person I thought you were."

They looked at each other for a long, silent moment. Neil wanted to say something more, something to make Penny understand a fraction of what he was feeling, of how sorry he was. But he couldn't go on. Finally, Penny opened the door and walked out of the school.

She'll never speak to me again, Neil told himself. *I don't blame her at all. I'm not the person I thought I was, either.*

He walked back down the hallway in a daze. He didn't know how he could get through the rest of the day, or the rest of the days of school to come. He felt completely alone.

Instead of going to his next class, Neil turned around and headed outside to the parking lot. He wasn't consciously cutting class. He just could not see himself being with people. Still feeling empty inside, he went to his car and got in.

But the energy to move was completely gone. He couldn't even start the car. He just sat there, staring into space.

An hour or so later, he suddenly realized someone was tapping on the glass next to him. Startled, he turned and saw Elizabeth standing outside his car. He slowly rolled down the window.

"I got permission to skip my study hall, so I could take galleys to the printer, and I saw you when I pulled into the parking lot. Are you OK?"

He just shook his head. "I don't know."

"Listen, Penny told me what happened. She's really upset," Elizabeth told him.

"Liz, I can't—"

"Wait, I want to tell you something," she cut in. "I was thinking about it. It's not like there's anything good about what you did. It was terrible. But I think it must have taken a lot of courage to tell Andy the truth."

Neil looked at her without speaking. Her eyes were sad and compassionate.

"I don't know why you did what you did," Elizabeth went on hurriedly. "But I can tell how awful you feel about it now. Sometimes it's easy to get mixed up. Lots of times we take things out on the people we care about the most."

He nodded and let his breath out in a long sigh. "Liz, I never meant to do it . . ."

"Maybe one little part of you did," she suggested. "And that part just took control for a second. I mean, I know you really care. I know you're not Charlie Cashman."

Neil's chin started to tremble, and he looked away in embarrassment. Elizabeth's sympathy hurt as much as Penny's scorn.

"And I think Penny knows that, too," Elizabeth went on. "It's just going to take a while for her to realize it. Once she gets over the hurt."

"I don't think so." He sighed. "She'll never forgive me. No one will."

Elizabeth looked down. "They might. I can't say anything for sure. But maybe the people who care about you will try to understand, and then maybe . . ."

"Oh, Liz." Neil shook his head. "How did it happen? I was such a fool. I just let Charlie sweep me along with him. I was as bad as he is."

"Don't do that to yourself," Elizabeth said. "It won't do any good to keep punishing yourself for what's already happened. The important thing is to make sure it doesn't happen again."

Neil looked at her, at a loss for words. He felt so grateful to her for trying to understand that he wanted to hug her. Elizabeth glanced away again and then gave him an uncomfortable smile.

"I have to go," she said gently. "Don't give up on Penny too quickly. And if you need to talk . . ."

He nodded, barely able to speak. "Thanks."

She straightened up and pulled the strap of her bag over her shoulder. "Bye."

Neil watched her walk toward the school. Then he drew a deep breath and started his car. He had a lot of thinking to do.

Neil drove aimlessly for some time. Eventually he found himself driving past the school again. As he passed the football field, he caught sight of a solitary figure walking across it. It was Andy.

Neil's stomach started churning. He pulled his gaze away and drove on by. More than anything, he wished there was some way to set things right.

Then he saw a group of people walking toward Andy from the other direction. In an instant, he realized it was Charlie and his gang. And Neil knew without a doubt that they were going to "teach Andy another lesson."

He didn't waste any time. Pulling over to the side of the road by the football field fence, he jumped out of the car. There was a gate a few yards farther along, and he headed for it, watching anxiously as the distance closed between Andy and the others.

"Andy!" he called, bursting through the gate and running toward him.

Andy turned and saw him. His face was stony while he waited for Neil to reach him.

"What? Didn't want to miss another chance?" Andy asked in a bitter voice. He put his horn case down and glared at Neil.

"No," Neil replied. He was trying to stay in control. "I'm standing with you this time."

"I don't need your kind of help," Andy muttered.

"I don't care." Neil faced him squarely. "I'm not going to stand by this time and watch you get beat up."

131

"Hey, Freemount, just in time!" Charlie yelled. He and his buddies laughed.

Neil held Andy's gaze. "I don't expect you to thank me or ever to like me again. But they'll have to beat me up, too, if they try something with you."

Breathing hard, Andy turned to watch the others come closer.

"You can still run, Jenkins," Charlie taunted. "Show us how fast you can run."

"I'm not running," Andy said. He raised his chin.

Charlie sauntered up and looked Neil over. "What's with you, Freemount?"

"Back off, Charlie," Neil warned. "I don't want to fight you."

"Oohoo!" Charlie arched his eyebrows and looked back at his friends. "He jumped to the other side of the fence again. You're a regular jack-in-the-box, Neil."

Charlie's tone was still threatening, but he was beginning to look doubtful. He seemed to be having second thoughts about taking on both Andy *and* Neil.

"If you touch me again, Cashman," Andy said, "I swear I'll see you in jail, with a lawsuit so big your folks will have to take it out of your hide."

"Oh, yeah?" Charlie's swaggering manner was losing some of its punch. "What makes you think I'd even waste my time on you, anyway?" he sneered.

"Come on, Charlie," Jerry McAllister said. "Let's blow."

Charlie stared hard at Andy for another long moment and then switched his gaze to Neil. "You'll be sorry, Freemount."

Neil laughed dryly. "I doubt it."

After another scornful stare, Charlie shrugged and waved to the others. "Let's get out of here."

They pushed past Andy and Neil and walked away.

Neil drew a long breath. His arms were shaking slightly at his sides. Neither he nor Andy spoke while the gang sauntered off. The silence between them was tense.

"You probably think this makes it even," Andy burst out suddenly. He glared at Neil. "But it doesn't."

"I know it," Neil agreed. He sighed. "And I know saying I'm sorry doesn't make any difference either, but I swear, I am. I'll never stop being sorry. And whether you want me to or not, I'll stand by you whenever Charlie gets the urge to break heads."

Andy looked away. He seemed tired and sad and most of all, alone.

"Why's it so hard?" he whispered, as though to himself.

There was no answer Neil could give. He wished there was, but he just couldn't find one. He hunched his shoulders inside his jacket and squinted against the sunlight.

"I guess I'll see you around," he said.

Andy picked up his French horn case. "Yeah. I guess."

They looked at each other for a long moment. Miles and miles seemed to stretch between them, and Neil knew they both regretted it deeply. Without another word, Andy started walking away.

Neil watched him for a few seconds, then headed back toward his car.

On Thursday evening, Penny sat at her desk, ignoring her homework. She was just beginning to get over the shock of Neil's confession. She felt hurt and betrayed, as well as mortified that she had misjudged him so badly.

"I thought I was smarter than that," she grumbled to herself.

Sighing, she stood up and went to the window. Then she sat on her bed. The first thing she noticed was the little book of poetry on her night table. It had been a birthday present from Neil.

She frowned but picked it up anyway. When he gave it to her, he was so sweet and bashful about it, because he said he wasn't sure she would like it. But she loved it, especially since he had picked it out. It was such a considerate present.

How could he be the same person who hit Andy? she wondered.

It seemed impossible. But the kind, thoughtful Neil she had always cared about so much *was* the same person. Something must have gone very wrong for him to do what he did, she realized sadly.

And she hadn't been able to help him figure it out. Penny felt a pang of guilt. Maybe she should have tried harder. She had kept telling Neil to try to understand Andy and be there for him, but maybe *she* should have been there more for *Neil*. Knowing how upset he was, maybe she could have done something to help. And then again, maybe not. Either way, she did owe it to him to try to understand. He had looked truly anguished the last time they spoke.

"Oh, I don't know," she said out loud. She

put the book down and stared into space. Downstairs, the telephone rang, and Penny heard her little sister answer it.

"Penny, for you! It's Neil!"

Penny's heart jolted. She cleared her throat. "Tell him—" She broke off and looked at the book of poetry again. "I'm coming," she called.

She stood up and squared her shoulders. She wasn't going to make any promises. But she would listen.

Elizabeth walked into the *Oracle* office Friday after school. Penny was there working on the final layout for Monday's paper, and Elizabeth joined her at the big table.

Penny looked up and smiled, but there was a preoccupied expression on her face. Elizabeth knew Penny and Neil had been having a hard time. Penny had confided that she wasn't sure if she could keep seeing Neil after finding out that he had hit Andy. Elizabeth still thought Neil was a good, caring person, but of course Penny would have to come to her own conclusions. Still, Elizabeth really hoped they didn't break up.

"How's everything going between you and

Neil?" she asked gently, a note of concern in her voice.

Penny looked at her friend thoughtfully for a moment before answering. "We're talking to each other now, at least. I'm still mad about what he did," she went on, "but I can't just cut him out of my life. I care about him too much to do that. . . ."

Elizabeth smiled. "I'm really glad to hear that. I'm sure everything will work out. Hey—I almost forgot," she added. "Guess what? Scott Trost is failing in two of his classes. He's going to be suspended from the football team."

"You mean we've lost another quarterback?" Penny said. "First Ken and now Scott. What are they going to do?"

"They'll have to have tryouts for a new quarterback," Elizabeth answered. Her blue-green eyes were dancing with excitement. "Penny, are you thinking what I'm thinking?"

Penny looked at her questioningly for a moment, then snapped her fingers as she understood. "Oh, right! You think that girl is going to try out for the position?"

"I don't know," Elizabeth said. She tapped a pencil against her palm. "But I'm dying to find out. And it would be big news if she does."

Penny smiled. "Any idea who it is?" she asked.

"Not a clue," Elizabeth admitted.

Penny frowned. "Well, if she does try out it might be a bigger story than we think," she observed.

"Why?"

"Think about it," Penny said. "Everybody assumes Ken will be quarterback, but with him just getting his sight back lately, he's not necessarily in perfect shape."

The girls knew Ken's eyesight still wasn't one hundred percent. If a girl did try for quarterback and if she *was* good, it could mean serious competition for him.

"I can hardly wait," Elizabeth said with a smile. "I bet the sparks will really fly!"

Will Ken Matthews face stiff competition at the quarterback tryouts?
Find Out in Sweet Valley High #70,
MS. QUARTERBACK.

COULD *YOU* BE THE NEXT SWEET VALLEY READER OF THE MONTH?

ENTER BANTAM BOOKS' SWEET VALLEY CONTEST & SWEEPSTAKES IN ONE!

Calling all Sweet Valley Fans! Here's a chance to appear in a Sweet Valley book!

We know how important Sweet Valley is to you. That's why we've come up with a Sweet Valley celebration offering exciting opportunities to have YOUR thoughts printed in a Sweet Valley book!

"How do I become a Sweet Valley Reader of the Month?"

It's easy. Just write a one-page essay (no more than 150 words, please) telling us a little about yourself, and why you like to read Sweet Valley books. We will pick the best essays and print them along with the winner's photo in the back of upcoming Sweet Valley books. Every month there will be a new Sweet Valley High Reader of the Month!

And, there's more!

Just sending in your essay makes you eligible for the Grand Prize drawing for a trip to Los Angeles, California! This once-in-a-life-time trip includes round-trip airfare, accommodations for 5 nights (economy double occupancy), a rental car, and meal allowances. (Approximate retail value: $4,500.)

Don't wait! Write your essay today.
No purchase necessary. See the next page for Official rules.

ENTER BANTAM BOOKS' SWEET VALLEY READER OF THE MONTH SWEEPSTAKES

OFFICIAL RULES:

READER OF THE MONTH ESSAY CONTEST

1. No Purchase Is Necessary. Enter by hand printing your name, address, date of birth and telephone number on a plain 3" x 5" card, and sending this card along with your essay telling us about yourself and why you like to read Sweet Valley books to:

READER OF THE MONTH
SWEET VALLEY HIGH
BANTAM BOOKS
YR MARKETING
666 FIFTH AVENUE
NEW YORK, NEW YORK 10103

2. Reader of the Month Contest Winner. For each month from June 1, 1990 through December 31, 1990, a Sweet Valley High Reader of the Month will be chosen from the entries received during that month. The winners will have their essay and photo published in the back of an upcoming Sweet Valley High title.

3. Enter as often as you wish, but each essay must be original and each entry must be mailed in a separate envelope bearing sufficient postage. All completed entries must be postmarked and received by Bantam no later than December 31, 1990, in order to be eligible for the Essay Contest and Sweepstakes. Entrants must be between the ages of 6 and 16 years old. Each essay must be no more than 150 words and must be typed double-spaced or neatly printed on one side of an 8 1/2" x 11" page which has the entrant's name, address, date of birth and telephone number at the top. The essays submitted will be judged each month by Bantam's Marketing Department on the basis of originality, creativity, thoughtfulness, and writing ability, and all of Bantam's decisions are final and binding. Essays become the property of Bantam Books and none will be returned. Bantam reserves the right to edit the winning essays for length and readability. Essay Contest winners will be notified by mail within 30 days of being chosen. In the event there are an insufficient number of essays received in any month which meet the minimum standards established by the judges, Bantam reserves the right not to choose a Reader of the Month. Winners have 30 days from the date of Bantam's notice in which to respond, or an alternate Reader of the Month winner will be chosen. Bantam is not responsible for incomplete or lost or misdirected entries.

4. Winners of the Essay Contest and their parents or legal guardians may be required to execute an Affidavit of Eligibility and Promotional Release supplied by Bantam. Entering the Reader of the Month Contest constitutes permission for use of the winner's name, address, likeness and contest submission for publicity and promotional purposes, with no additional compensation.

5. Employees of Bantam Books, Bantam Doubleday Dell Publishing Group, Inc., and their subsidiaries and affiliates, and their immediate family members are not eligible to enter the Essay Contest. The Essay Contest is open to residents of the U.S. and Canada (excluding the province of Quebec), and is void wherever prohibited or restricted by law. All applicable federal, state, and local regulations apply.

READER OF THE MONTH SWEEPSTAKES

6. Sweepstakes Entry. No purchase is necessary. Every entrant in the Sweet Valley High, Sweet Valley Twins and Sweet Valley Kids Essay Contest whose completed entry is received by December 31, 1990 will be entered in the Reader of the Month Sweepstakes. The Grand Prize winner will be selected in a random drawing from all completed entries received on or about February 1, 1991 and will be notified by mail. Bantam's decision is final and binding. Odds of winning are dependent on the number of entries received. The prize is non-transferable and no substitution is allowed. The Grand Prize winner must be accompanied on the trip by a parent or legal guardian. Taxes are the sole responsibility of the prize winner. Trip must be taken within one year of notification and is subject to availability. Travel arrangements will be made for the winner and, once made, no changes will be allowed.

7. 1 Grand Prize. A six day, five night trip for two to Los Angeles, California. Includes round-trip coach airfare, accommodations for 5 nights (economy double occupancy), a rental car -- economy model, and spending allowance for meals. (Approximate retail value: $4,500.)

8. The Grand Prize winner and their parent or legal guardian may be required to execute an Affidavit of Eligibility and Promotional Release supplied by Bantam. Entering the Reader of the Month Sweepstakes constitutes permission for use of the winner's name, address, and the likeness for publicity and promotional purposes, with no additional compensation.

9. Employees of Bantam Books, Bantam Doubleday Dell Publishing Group, Inc., and their subsidiaries and affiliates, and their immediate family members are not eligible to enter this Sweepstakes. The Sweepstakes is open to residents of the U.S. and Canada (excluding the province of Quebec), and is void wherever prohibited or restricted by law. If a Canadian resident, the Grand Prize winner will be required to correctly answer an arithmetical skill-testing question in order to receive the prize. All applicable federal, state, and local regulations apply. The Grand Prize will be awarded in the name of the minor's parent or guardian. Taxes, if any, are the winner's sole responsibility.

10. For the name of the Grand Prize winner and the names of the winners of the Sweet Valley High, Sweet Valley Twins and Sweet Valley Kids Essay Contests, send a stamped, self-addressed envelope entirely separate from your entry to: Bantam Books, Sweet Valley Reader of the Month Winners, Young Readers Marketing, 666 Fifth Avenue, New York, New York 10103. The winners list will be available after April 15, 1991.